MALPANI

THE
TENTH SON

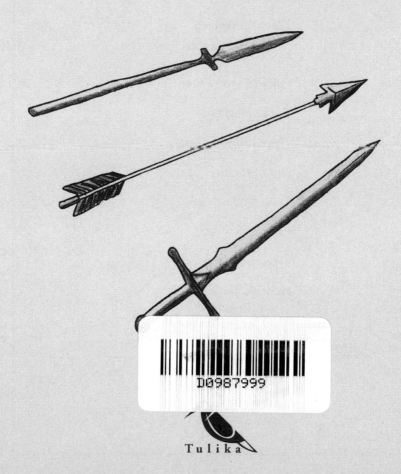

Tulika

CONTENTS

Broken

"Hey arrowhead, look over here," Liam's shout forced Advik to spin around. At that moment, Liam pulled the trigger on a water pistol he had poised right at Advik's pants. He and Jacob exploded into peals of laughter as Advik looked on, unamused.

"Oh no! What are you going to do now? Are you going to shoot an arrow at us? Oh, I'm so scared!" Jacob added.

"You got me, arrowhead." Liam slammed his fist on his chest like an arrow had hit him and fell to the ground laughing hard.

The passage that connected the main hallway to the playground was full of kids getting ready for recess. Advik looked around. It felt like the school had come to a standstill and everyone was staring at him.

Jacob wrenched Advik's backpack away from him and pulled out the bow and arrow set that Advik carried around with him. "Are you going to fight in *The Hunger Games?* Play a real sport, not some darts! Darts are for sissies!"

"Please leave my bow and arrows alone," Advik pleaded.

"Oh, are you worried about these toys? I'm going to fix them for good now." Sniggering, Jacob broke the bow in two with his hands and then destroyed the arrows.

The onlookers laughed. Tears rolled down Advik's cheeks. He thought about throwing a punch, but he didn't believe he had the size or strength to take on Liam and Jacob. The pair mocked and made crying faces at him, relenting only when they noticed a teacher heading in their direction.

Advik picked up his opened backpack and dragged his feet away from the crowd to his classroom, leaving behind the wreckage of his treasured bow and arrows. Humiliated and angry, he sat down at his desk and buried his face in his palms.

For Advik, a fifth-grader at Sherwood Elementary School, getting teased about his love for archery had become the norm. He had been introduced to the sport at the age of six by his grandfather, who told him the story of Karna, the supreme archer and invincible hero of the Mahabharata. He was fascinated, and asked for a bow and arrow for his seventh birthday. Since then, archery had become his whole world, and everything — even down to his doodles — was based on it

Apart from his classmates, he became the laughing stock of the boys who played football. They saw archery as nothing more than child's play. At first, Advik would tell himself to ignore their jibes and hurtful comments, but this didn't leave him any better off at present.

He didn't want to complain about it at home because, initially, the teasing was mostly benign. Things changed when the school bullies Liam and Jacob found out about it and started calling him 'arrowhead'.

Advik was an introvert. He didn't have any close friends in school, and he wasn't the kind who would go out and seek friendships either. Often he was found alone at the end of class lines, by himself, while all the others hung out together.

Advik didn't feel like doing anything for the rest of the day in school. He just wanted school to end and go home. For more than an hour, Ms. Connie noticed that Advik had his head down and was silent. As his teacher, she wanted to make sure he was doing alright.

"Is everything okay, Advik?"

Advik shook his head and resumed his forlorn position. Before Ms. Connie could persist, the bell rang. Advik seized the opportunity to quickly collect his things and make a mad dash for the stairs at the front entrance, where he found his dad waiting to take him home.

As soon as Shiv saw his son's face, he knew something was wrong.

"What happened? Are you okay? Did someone say something to you?"

"I don't want to talk about it right now." Advik kept his eyes on the ground as he walked wordlessly to the car Shiv, not protesting, followed, and began the drive home. After a few minutes, however, he heard quiet sobs coming from the back seat. He pulled the car over, turning around to look at Advik, who wished desperately to be invisible at that moment.

"Advik, I think we've gone far enough; will you please tell me what's wrong? Did something happen today?"

"I don't want to go to school anymore," Advik replied.

"I understand, but you need to tell me what happened before we take any drastic steps," Shiv tried to calm him. "How about you tell me about what happened in detail when we get home and then we can decide what is best. Okay?"

Advik agreed with a nod. Shiv texted Sanaa, Advik's mother, and they drove home without saying a word. As the garage door opened for the car, Sanaa rushed out to greet them.

For the next hour, Advik narrated the whole incident and how he felt about it. He also recounted every episode that had happened before and which, he felt, led to this moment. Shiv and Sanaa were both upset about what their son had been made to endure and couldn't believe that Advik had kept this all to himself.

By dinner time, they had managed to calm him down, and were determined to talk to the school administration and his class teacher about it. Advik fell asleep shortly after, exhausted.

Talking about the incident, Shiv and Sanaa decided that the next morning both of them would take him to school and have a chat with the principal. Sherwood Elementary and the school district had a zero-tolerance policy against bullying; even so, this string of incidents had gone on and on, unnoticed and unchecked.

Advik's fascination with archery was not new, and because he had become interested in Indian mythology, they had encouraged his interests. However, they were now forced to think about whether they should have nurtured a different interest altogether.

A scare in the night

In the dead of night, Shiv's cell phone began to ring. Sanaa woke him up to answer it.

"Your phone's ringing. Who's calling in the middle of the night?"

Shiv looked at the phone screen, noting that it was just five minutes past 1 am. It was his uncle Sunil calling from India. Shiv contemplated for a minute about whether or not to pick up the call. His dad's brother usually forgot the time difference between India and the US and was prone to calling at odd hours.

"Please answer. It may be an emergency," Sanaa advised. Shiv reluctantly picked up the phone and walked out of the master bedroom.

"Hello Chacha, is something wrong? You're calling us well after midnight."

"Shiv, it's about your dad."

"What happened to Papa?"

"He had a heart attack earlier this morning. We have admitted him to the hospital, but he is still critical. I think all of you should come home as soon as you can."

Shiv felt his heart rate spike and his blood run cold. His worst fear had come to life. He always worried about his dad, who lived alone in their ancestral home in Meerut. Shiv being the only child, he and Sanaa had tried, on several occasions, to convince him to come away with them to the USA but they were unsuccessful.

Shiv's father, Ramesh, liked spending time with his son's family in the USA, but he didn't like the lonely feeling when he was left to watch television and surf the net while the rest of the family was off at work and school. He missed his friends and social life in India. To start from the beginning in a new country at his age was nearly unthinkable.

Shiv understood this and finally gave up on convincing him, but he always worried about how his dad was doing. He was afraid of getting a phone call just like this one, in the middle of the night.

Sunil Chacha answered all his questions about his father's health but urged him to rush to India. Shiv hung up and walked back into the room where Sanaa waited to hear the full story.

"I heard bits and pieces of your call. What's happened?"

"Papa had a heart attack this morning, and he's in critical condition at the hospital." Shiv sat down on the floor next to the bed as he relayed everything in a worried voice. Disbelief and sadness clouded his eyes, and Sanaa, who had never seen this side of him before sprang into action. "You book tickets, and I'll start packing," she said. "We'll talk to Advik's school in the morning."

Shiv looked at Sanaa, glad that she was taking control. He did as he was told, rushing into his study to book tickets.

All the commotion woke up Advik. "Papa, is it time for school already?" he called out. "Can I sleep for one more minute?"

"Advik, go back to sleep. We will wake you when it's time," Sanaa replied as she opened the access door to the garage to pick up the travel bags.

"Okay, Mom," Advik replied and closed his eyes.

Grizzly on the aeroplane

Advik got up with a shock and looked at the alarm clock next to his bed. It was 9 am. He thought about school and then felt happy that his parents weren't sending him after what had happened the day before.

Suddenly, he remembered about the night, jumped out of bed and ran to his parents' bedroom. They were busy packing.

"What happened? Where are we going?"

Sanaa took a deep breath and beckoned to him.

"Advik, come sit here. We need to talk to you." Advik quietly sat down on the bed.

"We got a call late in the night that your Dadaji is sick and is in the hospital. We have to go to India to see him."

"Oh! Is it bad, Mom?"

"We don't know all the details yet. We'll know more when we get there."

"I hope he gets well soon." Advik saw that his parents looked exhausted and worried.

"I hope so too," Shiv said. "Why don't you get ready and pack your bag?"

"Okay, Papa." Advik started walking towards the bathroom but paused and turned back.

"What about my school, then?"

"I talked to your principal, and your absence will be excused because of the emergency."

"And —" Advik started to say something but stopped.

"And what? About what happened yesterday?" Shiv asked. Advik nodded his head. "I did talk to her about that, and she said we could look into it after we come back."

Advik nodded and disappeared into the bathroom.

A few hours later, a family friend dropped them at the airport.

Advik enjoyed watching movies on the entertainment system of the aeroplanes and his parents never limited his screen time on long flights. In a way, he was looking forward to the trip, though he was also worried about his Dada.

After they had boarded, Advik hugged his father. "Papa, it will all be okay." Shiv smiled and ruffled his hair, and they settled in for their long flight.

Advik had many fond memories of his Dadaji. Their conversations would go from listening to Indian mythological stories and made-up tales to arguing with one another. Dada, however, always paid attention to everything Advik had to say and answered all his questions.

Once, on a train ride from Delhi to Agra, Advik noticed that everything in the toilets was getting flushed down onto the tracks. First, he felt a little weird, but then he asked his grandpa, "Does the same thing happen in a plane? It would be gross to have poop fall on you from the sky as you are walking down the road." Both of them imagined how it would look and exploded with laughter.

Advik smiled to himself as he remembered that incident. His father gave him a puzzled look. Advik decided against letting him in on it. He slid the headphones over his ears and plugged them into the entertainment system.

Sanaa wrapped Advik in a blanket as he searched through kid-friendly movies. Once he'd figured out what he wanted to watch, he was set for the journey.

He was sleeping when the crew announced their descent into New Delhi airport.

"Wake up Advik; we are in India," his mother prodded him.

"One more minute, I'm sleepy," Advik responded, just as he would at home.

"We need to leave the airplane. You can go to sleep when we sit in the car."

"Can I please just —?" before Advik could complete his sentence, Shiv patted him on his butt. Advik was puzzled.

"We need to go now and escape your grizzly bear snores. Up now," his dad urged with a smile. Advik reluctantly got up and from under the seat, pulled his backpack, which accompanied him on all his journeys. They had finally arrived in India.

Pee monster strikes

Advik loved his Dada's old house built in black stone near the centre of town. His favourite place was the big wooden swing in the front courtyard where he used to sit for hours, either talking to his grandfather, or reading a book.

At the airport, they all got into a car that Sunil Chacha had arranged to take them to Meerut. It was still dark outside, and the two-hour journey after the exhausting flight was pretty painful; it felt like their travel was never-ending. Advik was zoned out, but then he saw the board that said 'Meerut-10'. Advik poked his dad.

"Papa only ten more miles… err no ten kilometers." Shiv laughed.

"You got that right, son; just a few more minutes and we'll be there." Advik sat up straight in his seat and looked outside anxiously.

As they finally entered Meerut from the highway, they saw that the town had begun to awaken for the day. A few chaiwalas had opened their shops and started to boil huge dekchis of tea. Doodhwalas with cans of milk clanging on their cycles were off to make the morning's deliveries.

The noise forced the cows and dogs sleeping on the street to open their eyes unwillingly. Advik looked on in amusement, while Shiv was reminded of his childhood.

As they started driving down West End Road, Advik noticed a giant white pillar that rose suddenly from the side of the road.

"Papa, what is that?" Advik asked.

"Oh, that one? I believe it is the Shaheed Smarak of Meerut. It is a memorial devoted to the martyrs of the First War of Independence in 1857."

"I don't know about that. Can you tell me the story?"

"Maybe later; we are about to reach home," Shiv said as the car approached Ghantaghar. Advik looked curiously at the magnificent orange brick clock tower and the vehicles passing through its gate. His favourite colour was orange. He turned back to look at the tower with wide eyes, even after they left it behind them.

The car then turned into the lane in the busy market area where their home was located. To Advik's surprise, two cows were blocking the entrance to the alley and didn't budge even when they saw the car coming.

The driver honked a couple of times, but the cows just sat there.

"Now what do we do, Papa?"

"I guess we'll have to make the cows move. Would you like to help?" Shiv said as he got out of the car, along with the driver.

"Sure," Advik responded. He threw a glance back at his mother, who didn't look as though she approved, but she didn't say anything to stop him. Shiv gave one of the comfortably settled cows a firm pat, startling it into standing.

The sudden movement of the large animal surprised Advik. He let out a loud screech. It further frightened the cow, making it pee.

"Yuck!" Advik shouted as he ran back to the car. Shiv and the driver started laughing. Advik sat on the back seat and checked to see if he had anything on him. Luckily he had managed to escape the pee monster.

He noticed that on the other side of the cow, a boy and a girl were standing and laughing at what they had just seen. They reminded him of the school bullies, and he clenched his fists.

"Pee attack!" the boy shouted. Advik glared at them with anger. Sanaa was watching quietly, but couldn't control her laughter either.

"This is just stupid. I want to go punch those kids in their faces for laughing at me," Advik fumed with his teeth clenched.

"What did you say?" Sanaa was quick to catch him.

"You're all laughing at me. You're all being mean! Just like what happened at school with Jacob and Liam!"

"We are not laughing at you, Advik. What happened with the cow and your reaction was funny! But you're right, we shouldn't laugh. No more laughs," Sanaa tried to calm him down. Meanwhile, the two cows decided to make way for the car, and the two kids ran away.

A few metres ahead, the car came to a complete stop in front of a house built with black stone. It had two beautifully carved black wooden doors that looked out onto a small, rectangular, open courtyard. A big wooden swing was on the right, and to the left, a short flight of stairs led to the living room. The door opposite the front entrance led to the kitchen and bedrooms beyond. They were home.

Need for a miracle

Everyone got ready in a jiffy. Together they drove to the The Heart Hospital of Meerut, which was about fifteen minutes away. The building was clean but chaotic, with nurses and doctors in their lab coats sprinting from wing to wing. Shiv checked at the front reception, and they climbed up to the third floor and turned right. Shiv spotted Sunil Chacha outside one of the private rooms and rushed to him.

"How's Papa?"

"He is sleeping. His vitals are stable now, but the doctors think that the heart is still weak and they need to continue to monitor it."

"Advik, can you sit near Dada while we go talk to the doctors?" Shiv was clearly worried and wanted to understand everything for himself.

Advik nodded and sat down on a sofa in the room. The others left to talk to the doctors. Advik looked at his grandfather. A jungle of tubes was attached to his body.

After about ten minutes, he started to feel bored sitting alone when, suddenly, he heard a soft rustling noise. He turned to the bed and saw that his grandfather had opened his eyes and was adjusting his position.

"Who is it?" he said in a weak voice.

"It's me Advik," he replied as he walked to the bed and hugged his grandfather.

"Oh! My young man! It is so good to see you. When did you get here? Why are you sitting alone?"

"Dadaji, we got here a few minutes ago. Ma and Papa went to talk to the doctors."

"Good, good. Come and sit next to me." Advik climbed onto the bed and sat next to his grandfather.

"Does it hurt with all the wires and tubes attached?" Advik asked as he gently touched a couple of them.

"Oh no, my son. Now that you are here, nothing hurts." He laughed weakly.

"Do you need to take more rest? I heard Papa say that the doctors want to keep on monitoring your heart."

"Well, let the doctors worry about all that. Enough about me. How is your school? Are you having fun? How was the journey?"

Advik paused for a few seconds and said, "I don't want to talk about school. The journey was okay."

"Now, that is not good. Is everything alright at school? Do your Mom and Dad know?"

"They know, but I don't want to talk about it."

"What else would you rather talk about?"

"Anything," Advik mumbled.

"What was that?"

"Nothing! Oh wait, I know," Advik remembered. "Papa mentioned something about the First War of Independence. There was a big white pillar we saw on the way from the airport. Papa told me that the government dedicated it to the First War of Independence."

"Oh, the Shaheed Smarak."

"Yes! That one, tell me more about it."

"It is a long story, and I am not sure how long I can talk. But let's start and see how far we get. Do you know who controlled India before independence?"

"In school, we learned that the British controlled most of India. They did that in America, too."

"Exactly, my dear. At first, it was not the British Empire, but a British company called East India Company that came to trade, but soon decided to meddle with local rulers and take over their kingdoms. Finally, in 1857, the Indians tried to throw out the British for the first time.

A revolt by the soldiers started it off, and that revolt began here, in Meerut. The Shaheed Smarak was built in their memory."

Shiv and Sanaa entered the room. Sunil Chacha had left to get some food for everyone. They saw Advik chatting with his grandfather.

"Papa, you are not supposed to talk, and the doctors have kept you under observation. Still, here you are, telling stories to Advik."

"Son, I am an old man. How many chances am I going to get to have an interesting chat with my grandson?" Before he could finish his protest, his breathing became shallow, and he clutched at his chest. Shiv rushed out of the room to call for a doctor.

Advik and Sanaa stood outside as the doctors and nurses hurried in and closed the door. Advik held on to his mother's hand tightly.

After fifteen minutes Shiv walked out with a tired, sad face.

"They will be moving him to intensive care. The doctors are saying that he may only have a few days. Only a miracle can save him now." All of them watched helplessly as Advik's Dada was moved to the intensive care unit on the fourth floor. Shiv followed the doctors and asked his wife and son to go home.

Three musketeers

On the way home, Advik didn't say anything. Once they got back, Sanaa tapped on his shoulder and asked him why he was so quiet.

"I am worried about Dada. If I hadn't forced him to tell me more about the 1857 war, he would have been okay."

"Don't blame yourself, Advik. Don't overthink what happened today. Why don't you go play and try to take your mind off it for a little while?"

Advik nodded and went and sat down on the swing. He noticed two heads popping up outside the front gate and their small eyes staring at him. He stared back at them and realised that those heads belonged to the two annoying kids who had laughed during the cow peeing episode. He frowned and looked the other way.

There was no movement for a few seconds, and suddenly, he saw the girl in a green butterfly dress step inside their yard. She paused for a second and then spoke.

"Hey, are you Dadaji's grandson? Aren't you the one who lives in America?"

Advik was not in a mood to talk. He didn't acknowledge the question and continued staring away.

"I know who you are. I think your name is something Vik," she said.

"It's Advik," he responded even though he didn't want to.

The girl said, "Oh yes! Your grandfather told us about you."

"You know my grandfather?" Advik looked at her, surprised.

"Yes, we do. In fact, Dadaji is one of our favourites. He tells us a lot of different stories. We live in this same lane, just a couple of houses down from here. We often play outside in the evenings, and that's when we see him sitting on the swing here and reading, or listening to music."

"Yes, he loves telling stories and sitting on this swing. You probably know more about him than I do." Advik smiled. The snobbish expression had vanished from his face.

"But he is sick, isn't he?" she asked as she stepped closer. Advik noticed the boy had followed her inside.

"Yes, he is in the hospital, and I am worried that I may have made his condition worse."

"What do you mean?"

Advik recounted the whole incident and told them how he was feeling sorry for making his grandfather tell him a story. Both of them had sat on the swing by this time.

"It's not your fault. I am sure he'll be okay," the boy added as he tapped Advik's shoulder. Advik looked at him. "My name is Samar and this is my twin sister Riya. We are ten years old," he added.

Samar was a slightly pudgy boy, who was dressed in black shorts with a red T-shirt. Riya was a slimmer girl who wore her long black hair in a ponytail. They both were smiling warmly at him.

"Aren't you the same kids who laughed at me when the cow peed close to my foot?"

"Yes. We didn't mean to laugh at you, but it was so funny. You don't see cows doing this in America, I suppose."

"That's for sure. But I hate it when people laugh at me."

"Sorry, we won't do it again. Next time you intend to do anything else that's hilarious just let us know in advance, and we'll make sure not to laugh." There was a playful air to Riya's voice, and Samar was still smiling. "But I hope that Dadaji gets well soon."

"I hope so too."

"Friends?" Samar asked and extended his hand.

Advik shook it and said "Yes!" Riya put her palm on top of their hands. Advik was glad that he had found friends his age, who weren't making fun of him and to whom he could talk openly.

"You know, almost every day after we finished playing we would come here and talk to Dadaji, and then he would make us wash our hands and feet and chant some prayers with him. It is that time again, and maybe we should do that. Who knows, maybe the gods will make him better after listening to our prayers," Riya suggested.

Advik wasn't convinced that it would work, but he decided to do it anyway.

Last resort

Sanaa looked up as Advik walked in with two other children in tow.

"Mom, meet my new friends. He's Samar and she's Riya. They live two houses down from here, and they know Dada very well. He has even taught them how to chant prayers, so I am going to do it with them today." The three children folded their hands and bowed their heads.

"That is an excellent idea. How about I get you something to eat after you finish your prayers?" Sanaa said, and walked towards the kitchen.

They all headed into the prayer room, which was always lit and beautifully decorated with idols of Lord Krishna and Lord Ganesha facing west. Samar lit an oil lamp while Riya lit an incense stick.

"When you pray, wish that your grandfather gets better soon and we will, too," Riya said as she folded her palms and closed her eyes.

Advik did the same.

"Dear gods," he prayed, "Please help my Dada get better. I will do anything you ask if you make him okay again."

Advik opened his eyes slightly and sneakily peered around at Samar and Riya, who still had their heads bowed. Not wanting to stand out, Advik closed his eyes again. He was beginning to get impatient, when he heard his mother call out for them.

"Kids, come to the kitchen after you finish."

Everyone opened their eyes, unfolded their hands, got up and ran to the kitchen. Sanaa had made a snack that quickly disappeared into their hungry bellies.

After eating, the three children went out to the swing and talked some more. A little later, they heard someone call for Samar and Riya.

"Oh, that must be Ma calling us. We must go now. We'll see you tomorrow." Samar hopped off the swing and beckoned to Riya, who reluctantly followed.

"Don't you guys have school?"

"It is summer break."

"Lucky you, I had to miss school. Not that I was super excited about attending school anyway," Advik replied with a shrug.

"Why?" Samar was curious.

"Some other time." Advik wasn't ready to tell everything just yet. Riya and Samar waved their goodbyes and excused themselves.

Sanaa walked out and stood next to the swing where Advik still sat. "They seem like nice kids. I'm glad that you found someone to talk to here."

"Yes, mom. Riya also told me that I should ask for Dada to get better when we were praying, so I did. I said I was ready to do whatever it takes to make him better."

"That was nice of you. I'm hopeful the gods will

answer our prayers. Go on now and do some reading. I'll check with Papa to see if there's an update."

"Can I play on my iPad?"

"You can try if you like, but I'm not sure if there's Wi-Fi here. If you can't connect, you should do some reading."

Advik ran to the room where he had kept his stuff and found his iPad. He switched it on and checked for Wi-Fi signals, but there were none. All his games were Wi-Fi enabled and it seemed he was out of luck.

For the next fifteen minutes, he fiddled with the calculator app. Finally, he got bored and picked up the book he had been reading.

He opened it and walked toward the bed in the room and lay down to read it. After some time and without realising it, Advik drifted off to sleep, the book still clutched firmly in his hands.

Sanaa, who had walked in to check on him, quietly took it from his hands, pulled the blanket over him and turned off the light. Darkness soon overtook the room and the little mosquito repellent that doubled as a night light went to work.

Celestial visitor

Advik was awakened in the middle of the night by a bright, peaceful white light. As his eyes fluttered open, he saw the silhouette of a person standing in the centre of his room. Thinking he might be dreaming, he pinched his face. The sting he felt in his right cheek let him know this was real.

Now terrified of the luminous intruder, Advik tried to scream for his parents. However, no sound came out. The one thing he could seem to control was the overwhelming urge to rush to the bathroom. As his eyes adjusted to the light, he noticed that the figure in his room was smiling at him.

"Narayan, Narayan! There is no need to be afraid, my son," said the man in a calming voice.

Advik looked carefully at the strange-looking man. His hair was matted, with flowers in it. He was wearing a saffron-coloured dhoti with a stole to match and some floral garlands. The most striking thing was what he was holding in his hand. It was a giant instrument that looked like a strange guitar.

Though he couldn't explain why, Advik felt he didn't need to fear the odd-looking man in his room. Still, he was uncomfortable. Finally, he took a deep breath and spoke.

"Who are you? What are you doing in my room in the middle of the night?"

"You have a lot of questions, Advik."

"How do you know my name?"

"Oh, another question. Well, I know the names of all who live in the universe." The man paused for a while. "To answer your first questions: my name is Narada, and I am here because you called me."

"Narada? Are you the one from my Dada's stories? Are you real?"

"You were listening! Good!" His smile was bright. "I am the one from your Dada's stories."

"I'm pretty sure I've never called you... Like, ever. Why are you carrying a giant... instrument?"

"Oh! Are you talking about my veena? It has a name too. I call it Mahathi. Would you like to see it?" Narada stretched out his hand.

"No, thank you. Why are you dressed like that? Like a girl."

"Well, close your eyes, count to three and open them again." Narada remained cheerful.

Advik closed his eyes, counted to three and opened his eyes again. He couldn't believe what he saw. Narada was smiling at him, wearing jeans and a T-shirt. The flowers and the veena had disappeared. His matted hair had turned into a ponytail.

"Narayan, Narayan! Now, is this okay for you?"

"I wish I could do that when getting ready for school. Then I could sleep until the last minute. You need to teach me how to do it!"

"Well, we will have to see about that." Narada smiled.

"You said I called you. When and how did I do that?"

"Do you remember the prayer you said this evening with your friends?"

"Yes I do, but how do you know about that?"

"As you know from the stories, I am the messenger of the gods. I am here to deliver a message from them. The gods need your help."

Advik's heart leaped into his throat. "I'm only ten. What can I do that the gods need? How come the gods themselves can't do it?" His confusion was visible on his face.

"Ah see, the catch is that I can't tell you the details until you agree. You have some thinking to do and a decision to make. I will also let you in on something else. Helping the gods will definitely force them to answer your prayers."

"How do I know that the gods can really heal my grandfather? And that they will?"

"Well, there are no guarantees, but do you have any reason to doubt the gods?"

"No, but then I've never done something like this before."

"I will also tell you this: if you agree to help, it will ensure the survival of many, many lives. Not just your Dada's."

"Can you give me some time to think?"

"Of course, but I say you should think wisely and quickly as time is of the essence. When you're ready, fold your hands and say 'Narayan, Narayan' and I will come right away." Narada gave Advik a kindly smile and slipped into the white light.

The room returned to darkness. The dim night light looked feeble in comparison to Narada's glow. Advik thought for a moment that he must have dreamed his conversation with the messenger of the gods. He looked around the room and nothing seemed out of place.

It was indeed strange. Advik laid his head back on his pillow, remembering the conversation over and over. Somewhere in the middle, he drifted into sleep, though the memory continued to replay.

You're bluffing!

Advik awoke early the next morning and hopped out of bed with no desire to 'sleep just one more minute' as he so often did. He followed the sounds of his parents' voices into the kitchen.

"How's Dada doing now?"

"Oh Advik, you're up early today. It looks like jet lag is kicking in for someone," Shiv smiled and continued, "Dada is doing the same as yesterday. There is no change. I wish I had good news for you."

Sanaa and Shiv exchanged glances, and she indicated that Shiv should not divulge any further information.

"Go brush your teeth and come back for breakfast," Sanaa changed the subject.

While Advik brushed his teeth, he considered whether he should tell his parents about his talk with Narada. He decided they wouldn't believe him and returned to the kitchen table.

"We should hurry and get ready," Shiv said, gobbling up the last of his breakfast. They waited till the household help, Shanta, arrived.

"Advik, we have to go to the hospital. Shanta is here to keep an eye on you. But she may have to step out to get some vegetables. You stay here and play. I heard you made new friends who are going to meet you today. Don't go out of the house."

He silently nodded.

After his parents left, Advik didn't know what to do. He went to his room and picked up the spare bow and arrow set that he had left in India on his previous visit, and went out to the courtyard. He shot some arrows aimlessly and missed every target he had in mind. Noticing Samar and Riya outside the house, he decided to tell them about Narada's visit. He waved his hand, and they ran right over. Shanta left the house but not before warning the children not to leave the house.

"I have to tell you both something."

"What is it?" Riya asked with a puzzled face.

Advik recounted the whole incident from the night before. The twins listened carefully.

"… And now I don't know what to do," Advik concluded. "I don't think my parents are going to believe me if I tell them," he added, with his heart beating fast. Samar and Riya looked at each other. Then they exploded into laughter, and Advik's faced turned red.

Riya, seeing his reaction, tried to control herself by holding her palm over her mouth, but Samar kept on laughing.

"It is a nice story, Advik, and I admire you telling it with a straight face. But you're bluffing," Riya blurted as she continued to chuckle. Advik clenched his fists and tightened his jaw. Samar, finally seeing the look on his face, sobered and addressed him seriously.

"Advik, it had to be a dream. There is no way you saw Naradamuni last night, and there's no way the gods asked for your help. Why you? Why not me? Did you pinch yourself? Honestly, the whole thing sounds crazy!"

"Of course I pinched myself to make sure that I wasn't dreaming. I don't know why me but you have to believe me! Why is this so hard? Okay look," Advik said, suddenly remembering what Narada had told him about summoning him.

He closed the doors of the house. He folded his palms and closed his eyes. Before he could utter a word, however, there was a SPLAT! sound, followed by the cawing of a raven flying over the courtyard. Advik opened his eyes in horror to see that a raven had flown overhead, leaving droppings on his folded hands.

"Foooew!" Samar and Riya burst out laughing again.

Advik, enraged, decided it was more important to focus on proving himself to his friends. He shook the droppings off his palms with a twitch. He closed his eyes once more, folded his palms and uttered the words.

"Narayan, Narayan!"

The courtyard illuminated for a fraction of second and Narada appeared in regular clothes in front of them. His ponytailed hair still gave away who he was — no veena or flowers were needed. Samar and Riya, thinking this was some ghost or black magic, ran to hide behind a pillar, staring in total disbelief.

The tenth son

Advik stood there with his hands folded, grinning at the messenger who now stood before him.

"Samar and Riya, there is no reason to be scared and hide," said Narada with a smile.

Samar and Riya slowly stepped out from behind the pillar holding each other's hands. Their faces were a mixture of fear and excitement.

"How do you know our names?"

"He knows everything about everyone. After all, he is the messenger of the gods. You know that," Advik smirked.

"Have you made your decision, my son?" Narada asked.

Advik paused for a second and replied. "I've decided that I will do what the gods want me to. You have to tell me exactly what I'm going to be doing, though."

"Fair enough, but think twice before you say yes. There is no going back on a promise to the gods."

"It doesn't really matter what it is, so long as it will help my Dada get better."

"As you wish, Advik, but first things first. I'll tell you why the gods have chosen you. It's a long story, so get comfortable."

Advik, Samar and Riya sat on the swing and listened. A hush fell over the courtyard, only the creaking of the swing was audible.

"Narayan, Narayan! How well do you know the Mahabharata?"

"I know a little bit from the stories that my Dada told me. Maybe Samar and Riya know more." The two nodded their heads in agreement.

"The Pandavas won the Kurukshetra war against the Kauravas. This victory came at a very high price. None of their sons survived the war. It was a grim beginning for the Pandavas, to say the least. They found out that Karna, the general of the Kaurava army and the great archer, was, in fact, their older brother. Karna and nine of his sons also perished in the war. Vrishaketu, the tenth son of Karna, survived. At the time, Vrishaketu was only a small child, who believed that no one could conquer his great father. The war, however, filled him with great darkness."

"What happened next?" Samar asked with wide eyes.

"Vrishaketu vowed to destroy Arjuna who had taken the life of his father, but when he faced him, he saw that Arjuna was repentant and mourned the death of Karna. From then on, Vrishaketu and Arjuna formed a special bond.

"Seeing his dead sons in Vrishaketu, Arjuna grew fond of him and took it upon himself to teach him everything he knew. Vrishaketu adopted the new family and began his training in archery under the guidance of Arjuna and Lord Krishna, who was impressed by his progress. Vrishaketu also mastered the invocation and use of various astras, or weapons."

"That must be really cool. I wish I could do that," Samar cheered with excitement.

"It is good to dream," Advik added a snarky comment.

"Careful what you wish for," Narada smiled and continued. "As the end of the era became clear in Lord Krishna's mind, he started to worry that these astras might fall into the wrong hands in the future and cause havoc.

"He asked Vrishaketu to promise that he would not use the Pashupatastra, the most destructive weapon that belonged to Lord Shiva. He also requested that he never pass on the knowledge of it to anyone. Vrishaketu promised that he wouldn't use the weapons, nor would he take any disciples. However, he made one request to Lord Krishna. He asked that someone from his lineage, with a pure heart, be able to invoke the astra by chanting the mantra in case of dire need.

"Lord Krishna agreed to his wish but asked him to conceal the mantras from prying eyes. Vrishaketu created a complicated treasure map to them that has since been unsolvable. That is the story of Karna and his tenth son." Narada took a long pause and looked at the children, who sat there wide-eyed and captivated.

Riya piped up, "But why are you asking for Advik's help? He doesn't even live in India. Is he some kind of half-blood like Harry Potter?"

"Good question, Riya. It just so happens that Advik here comes from Vrishaketu's lineage. He asked for help from the gods with a pure heart and offered to do what it takes. The gods believe he is the only one who can invoke the Pashupatastra."

"But why do we need the Pashupatastra?" Riya was still unsure.

"I see Advik is not the only inquisitive one here!" Narada smiled. "Get ready for another story." He took a deep breath.

"A while ago, the adviser to the gods left the council after Indra, the king of gods, insulted him. The gods could no longer effectively fight their foes, the asuras. They found a new adviser — Vishwa — who helped them defeat the asuras. Vishwa's mother, however, was an asura. Bowing to her pressure to help the demons, he secretly worked against the gods.

"Lord Indra killed Vishwa for his betrayal. Vishwa's father sought revenge against Indra. He lit a holy fire and prayed to Lord Shiva. From the fire rose the dragon-headed Harkasura, with a blood-chilling growl. His body shone like molten copper. His eyes were as fiery as the blazing sun, and from his lungs billowed flares of fire. A spiky mane ran along the length of his back, at the end of which swished a mighty tail. His body was covered in scales that glistened in metallic colours and his strong, sharp claws drew in and out, as though waiting to sink into an enemy. He held a trident in his right hand and stood tall on his two powerful legs.

Narada continued the story after a brief pause. "Vishwa's father ordered Harkasura to attack Indra. The demon attacked and swallowed him. The gods asked for Lord Shiva's help to get rid of Harkasura, and he used his weapon — the Pashupatastra — to kill the demon and free Lord Indra. However, before he died, Harkasura asked forgiveness from Lord Shiva and requested that if he were to be reborn, no gods could kill him. Only a human could, and with the celestial weapon, the Pashupatastra. Unfortunately, Lord Shiva granted his wish."

"Is Harkasura reborn or something?"

"Narayan, Narayan! Let me finish." Narada smiled. "After suffering a humiliating defeat by the gods and losing Harkasura, the asuras retreated to the subterranean realm of Rasatala where they tried to resurrect Harkasura," Narada continued with caution in his voice.

"The gods have seen the asuras make several failed attempts at the resurrection, but believe that they're getting closer to succeeding. Once Harkasura is revived, he will have a strength the gods won't know how to fight.

"The demons know they can't fly and attack Swargaloka, so they will break through to Bhuloka from Rasatala and enslave humans. The gods will be forced to fight to save humanity and will get annihilated by Harkasura in the process. The only weapon that can be used to vanquish him once more is the Pashupatastra."

"So are you saying the weapon is powerful enough to kill Harkasura, but since Lord Shiva granted Harkasura's wish that no god can kill him, it is up to me to invoke the weapon and defeat the demon?" Advik said, coming to a realisation.

"You are smart, Advik. You got it right. Narayan, Narayan!" Narada smiled.

"Are you going to help us fight?" asked Advik.

"Well, I am just the messenger. I can help with what you need, but I can't fight along with you or tell you what to do. If you ask me a question, I will guide you and provide as much information as I can."

"Do you think a ten-year-old can battle the most dangerous asura when even the gods can't?"

"You know, sometimes you don't need extraordinary strength to do great things. All you need is a strong belief."

"I want to help, but I'm not sure I can do it. I don't even know how to fight. If I could, I wouldn't have been bullied in my school."

"You leave that to me. I will teach you how to fight. You must believe that you can do this; believing in yourself right now is essential. The fate of this world rests in your hands, Advik. If you agree to all of this, we will start your training right away. There is so very little time to waste."

"Advik, if you say yes to this, we will help you," Riya pleaded. Advik thought for a moment.

"Okay, let's do this together; let's show the demons their place," Advik said as he extended his arm. Samar and Riya joined hands with him.

"We're going to need a place to train where no one can see us. Do you know of any?" Narada asked.

"I have an idea. Dada has an underground cellar! It has a secret door, and no one will ever think to look there for us," Advik replied, all charged up.

"Alright, then we will start tomorrow," Narada added, and disappeared.

Out of the fire

For a very long time, the subterranean realm of Rasatala was a dense forest with tall trees, where the rays of the sun didn't dare to touch the ground. Rasa Ganga was the only river that flowed through the realm.

After losing the battle with the gods, the asuras retreated to Rasatala, bringing destruction. Despite making it their home, they cut down trees in the forest that gave shade and shelter to the animals. They hunted everything that moved to satisfy their never-ending hunger. They changed the course of the river towards their settlements by blasting a mountain that helped change the flow. Apart from the asura settlements, the land now looked barren.

The demons frequently fought against each other and needed new weapons for their battles. They gouged out mounds and mounds of land on the outskirts of their settlements to mine metals required to forge these weapons, and left huge craters behind. The forges that heated the metals emitted toxic smoke, and the discoloured water used for cooling the weapons was dumped in the river that had turned grey. Nothing green could survive in the smoke-filled air. The realm suffered greatly after they had made it their home.

All that they thought about was revenge against the gods. But they didn't have a single leader who could lead them in battle. Three powerful demons, Tiraka, Virata and Sambara, continued to fight each other, causing more destruction.

Tiraka, the bull-headed demon, was the burliest among them. He could run for miles without stopping, and his curved horns were his greatest weapons. His head was useful for ramming through twenty trees at once, but it wasn't very good for strategy and leadership.

Virata was a true giant, who stood twenty feet tall. He was strong enough to uproot trees with his bare hands, and he was the only one who could fight one on one against Tiraka. But his biggest disadvantage was he had the head of a small raven and terrible eyesight. He struck fear into the hearts of all who crossed his path, but the other demons still laughed behind his back because he couldn't see the dangers that were close to him.

Sambara was the smartest of all the demons. His boar-shaped head with two metal rings in his nose made him look fierce, but he relied more on his brains than strength when it came to fighting. Knowing that his power couldn't measure up to Tiraka or Virata, he decided to build a fort for himself. The black ironstone fortress was impenetrable, and he could launch attacks from within it. Ironstone was a particular rock found only in the quarry under the fort that Sambara had strategically built above. After years of continued infighting that robbed the realm of its resources and drained the demons of their strengths,

Sambara made a decision. It was time they buried the hatchet, preserved what resources they could and made a collective effort. He invited Tiraka and Virata to his fort to discuss this, but they were understandably suspicious about his offer.

The ironstone fort, which had withstood numerous sieges led by Tiraka and Virata, was a formidable structure. Tiraka and Virata entered, still suspicious of Sambara's motives in inviting them.

They were pleasantly surprised to find nothing more than civilised conversation awaiting them and a plea for a united effort against the gods. Together, they stood a chance of bringing their foes to their knees. They knew that the asuras had the gods on the ropes when Harkasura had attacked them. If it hadn't been for that last-ditch effort from Lord Shiva, Harkasura would have been the ruler of the universe.

They discussed Harkasura's last wish and decided that if they could resurrect him, they could unite all asuras to fight against the gods, and no one could stop them. In the end, they all agreed to the new strategy.

United, the three made several attempts to revive Harkasura, but they were unsuccessful. After some time, Sambara suggested they capture a tantrik named Mahakala, who was the priest of Kamakhya temple, in the north-east of India. People believed that he had mastered the art of resurrection.

Sambara and Virata devised and carried out a plan to capture Mahakala, his wife and their son from their house. At first, he refused to help the asuras. When Tiraka killed his wife before his eyes and threatened to do the same to his son, he relented.

Mahakala got them to cut down tree after tree to build a two-storey-high fire, which crackled in the middle of the ironstone fort. Into this fire, he made offerings to the chants of Mrit Sanjeevani mantra that could bring the dead back to life.

As the intensity of his chants grew, blue smoke appeared in the middle of the fire. It swirled through and seemed to flow back into itself, solidifying in the centre of the roaring flames. The three asuras looked on in excitement.

A reptilian figure began to form in the blue smoke and, before long, emitted a deafening growl. From the flames, out stepped a fearsome creature, with the head of a dragon, dressed in warrior's clothing and wielding a trident. Red, blazing eyes stared at the three asuras before him. They dropped to their knees and bowed humbly.

The creature stood towering over the three demons, his long tongue playing on his jagged teeth. With smoke billowing from his nostrils, he pounded the hilt of the trident on the stone floor.

Harkasura had returned!!

"Welcome to Rasatala, Lord. We are blessed to have you back," Sambara spoke, his voice quivering.

"I am here to avenge my death and restore the glory and pride of the asuras. I will destroy the gods and anyone who stands against me. Our time to rule this universe has come," his rasping voice boomed through every corridor of the fortress.

"Hail Lord Harkasura!!" all three cheered. Other, lesser asuras, who had been standing guard, joined in exultant worship, along with Mahakala.

Training day

Since there was no time to lose, it was critical for the children to gain as much knowledge about the techniques of combat as they could in just a short time. The more they knew and the more they could train, the better equipped they would be in battle.

The following day, Sanaa took Advik to the hospital to visit his Dada. He was asleep because of the medicines. They watched him from behind the glass doors of the ICU. Advik was anxious to see if he would wake up, but he continued to sleep peacefully.

As his mother got up, saying they should leave, Advik whispered slowly, "Rest now Dada, I will take care of everything, and you'll be better soon. You'll see." In spite of no response from his grandfather, Advik felt that he had heard his message.

When they returned home, Advik settled himself on the swing. Samar and Riya, having spotted him getting into the house, quietly rushed to his side.

"We've been waiting for you all morning. When are we supposed to start our training with Naradamuni? Do you have weapons for us to use? Will Naradamuni be bringing them? What kind are we using?" Advik looked at them with a mix of amusement and irritation as he was bombarded with questions.

"Pipe down! I'll tell my Ma we're going to play. Wait here." Riya and Samar nodded their heads in agreement.

"Ma, I am going out to play with Riya and Samar," Advik yelled loudly.

"Okay, don't go too far though," Sanaa replied from inside.

"Okay, that's good. Let's figure this out," Advik said to his friends.

"Should we go to the cellar? Where is the secret door?" Samar was bursting with excitement.

"We might be able to make it to the door without anyone noticing," Advik replied. He took both of them to the living room by jumping over the four steps from the courtyard to the door. Advik opened one window and asked Samar to open the other.

Light flooded into the room. The multicoloured chandelier made the place look magical. On the right ran a wall with one small door that led to the kitchen. On the opposite wall was a large two-door cupboard, painted green. An old sofa stood in front, blocking it.

"Help me move the sofa," Advik said. With Riya and Samar, he pushed it far enough for him to open one of the doors. Inside, were two shelves. Beneath the lowest shelf was a small, hidden door. Advik opened it, revealing nothing but darkness. They could see a short flight of stairs.

"Come on guys, let's go." Riya and Samar hesitated. "No need to worry about the dark. I have been down here a bunch of times." The twins reluctantly stepped inside the large cupboard.

The stairs going down were steeper than average, so they had to jump from one step to another, but it was fun going down this way. Samar felt like they were entering a secret world that no one had seen before, and it felt wonderfully adventurous.

As they climbed down, the living room light became distant. Advik paused on the stairs for a couple of seconds, reaching to the right for a switch that he remembered was there.

A lone bulb lit up and brightened the rectangular room that matched the living room in size, but had no windows.

"Here it is! The secret underground room. What do you think?" Advik asked Samar and Riya.

"Awesome! This is cool. I don't think we can hear anything happening above, nor can anyone hear anything we are doing down here," Samar replied. Riya nodded in agreement.

"That's good. Let's get Naradamuni and start the training."

Advik folded his hands and uttered, "Narayan, Narayan!" Riya and Samar folded their hands too.

The shining white light filled the room, and Narada appeared with a big cloth bag tied with a rope, which he promptly dropped on the floor.

"Aaaah! This bag is heavy. I didn't know what weapons you kids want to learn to use, so I brought them all. Go ahead, take a look and make your choice. We will begin shortly."

All three ran to the bag and pulled the string to open it. It contained every weapon the children could imagine and several that they couldn't. The weapons looked small. Advik was the first one to pick up the bow and the arrow quiver. The bow grew in size once he picked it up, and adjusted itself to his grip.

Samar settled for a sword, which shot up to be the right size for him. He held it, gazing in amazement.

After several moments of indecision, Riya settled on the spear. She held it in her right hand, and the spear grew to fit her grip and size.

"Now then, are you all certain you want to use the weapons you've chosen?"

"Yes, Muni," the kids replied together.

"Very well then. These are special weapons. When you pick them up, they will grow to match your size, but when you drop them, they will return to being small." Narada closed his eyes and chanted something. Suddenly the wall before them split, and two dark hairy hands with long nails appeared from inside it, pushing the crack wide open. A repulsive creature entered the room. Burning red eyes buried within an angry face, large jagged teeth jutting from a prominent, wide jaw, and a huge, bulging figure made the asura look ferocious.

"What's stopping you now? Use your weapons and see how well you can defend yourselves from a creature like this."

As the asura marched towards them, Advik pulled an arrow from his quiver and shot at him. He was anxious, and his aim was off, keeping the arrow from reaching its full force. The demon grabbed it with one hand and broke it in two. Samar lunged out with his sword, and the beast swiftly took hold of that too, flinging it back at him. The sword hit the corner of Samar's shorts and pinned him to the wall. Riya's spear was the only thing that struck the asura, but it did very little damage.

Before Advik had a chance to pull out a second arrow, the demon grabbed him and Riya and pushed them against the wall. They all looked at each other helplessly. He looked everyone in the eye. Riya closed her eyes in fear. Samar was on the verge of wetting his pants. Advik was frozen — memories of the school bullies flooded his mind. Then Narada snapped his fingers, the demon vanished, and the room returned to normal.

The three breathed a sigh of relief and looked at Narada. It was a pretty scary way to begin the training, for sure. Their hearts were still beating fast.

"Narayan, Narayan! That was just a little taste," said Narada. "The real ones are going to be worse. That one was nothing more than an illusion. Now you know what to expect! You need to focus."

"I can't do this. I don't think I can fight," Advik said with tears in his eyes.

"Why not?" Riya asked sympathetically. Close to tears, Advik told them all about the bullies in school, and how he hadn't been able to stand up to them. He didn't think he had it in him to fight them or the demons. Samar and Riya patted him on his back.

"Don't worry about it now, Advik. We are with you, and together we can fight the demons. You have to remember that we are doing this for your grandfather and to save the world from Harkasura," Riya tried to boost Advik's confidence. "You know what? You should use that anger for the bullies in fighting the asuras."

"She's right, Advik. You can do it! Now, since we don't have much time, I am going to teach you how to increase your focus by chanting a mantra to goddess Saraswati — the Saraswati-Gayatri Mantra, which asks her to remove all obstacles in your learning. Say it after me, and try to feel the power of the mantra," Narada said and closed his eyes.

ॐ वाकदेव्यै च विद्महे।
ब्रह्मपत्न्यै च धीमहि।
तन्नो वाणी प्रचोदयात्।।

Om Vaakdeviyai cha Vidhmahe.
BramhaPathniyai cha Dheemahi.
Thanno Vaani Prachodayaath.

The kids repeated the mantra with their eyes closed. "Say it eight times, and make sure that you are saying it right. Then we'll try another asura," Narada smiled as he continued. The kids followed the orders carefully.

Narada snapped his fingers again. As the front wall began to fall apart, they chanted the mantra once more and took aim.

A huge and terrible asura lunged towards them, but they stood ready. Thwack!! Two arrows hit the asura in the chest one after the other. The demon tried to pull them out, but this time they had struck deep.

Seizing the opportunity, Riya hurled her spear with all force towards him. It hurtled through the air with a rhythmic, menacing whir and as it struck him, he let out a loud, blood-curdling scream.

Samar looked at Advik and winked. Advik got down on all fours. Samar climbed on him and jumped high to deliver a final blow to the demon with his sword. Blood spurted through the air as the steel cut through the neck of the monster, and he slumped to the ground.

The three stood stunned by what they'd just

accomplished. They looked at one another for a moment before bursting into cheers for their victory. Narada smiled and snapped his fingers. The asura disappeared, and the wall got back to normal.

"This is a good start, children. But we can't get too happy with a minor win and lose sight of our main goal. This is only the beginning. You must continue to know your strengths and work together as you just did."

Narada opened the palm of his right hand and what looked like a box wrapped in orange cloth appeared on it. The kids looked at each other, confused. But, with his signature smile, Narada said, "Narayan, Narayan! This is the book of mantras that will help you in your quest. I know Advik can't read the book written in Sanskrit, but Riya and Samar, you can help him."

The kids, enthused by their latest victory, smiled at one another. Advik took the book, and Narada disappeared. Riya and Samar thumped his shoulders and followed him up the stairs and out of their training chamber.

At night, Advik untied the orange cloth to reveal an ancient book of mantras. It had a copper cover with a picture of the Sun carved into it. He turned the cover and found that the pages were made of a light metal, with letters etched onto them. He recognised a few letters but nothing further. He wrapped it back and slid it under his pillow before falling asleep.

Over the next two days, Shiv and Sanaa found Advik hardly asking to play with electronic devices or complaining about boredom. They did notice more bruises and scrapes on his legs, but when he didn't complain about them, they didn't give it much thought, and put those down to his playing outside and being a kid!

Little did they know that their son's training in weaponry was advancing by the hour, and that somewhere within himself, Advik was finding the confidence to face the demons he had been scared of for a long time.

Pashurivas

Harkasura had gained control of Rasatala, and every demon in the realm had pledged allegiance to him. He appointed Tiraka, Virata and Sambara as his deputies. He struck down anyone who opposed him. His weapon, the trident, was the most feared in the realm.

After taking over Sambara's ironstone fort, Harkasura had ordered that every mace and sword that had been forged for his army be taken back, and tridents be given in their place. The asura army started their training with this new weapon. It was only a matter of time before they were all ready to march on Bhuloka and take it over.

Harkasura knew that the only thing that could stop him this time was the Pashupatastra. The invocation mantra had long since been lost, but he believed that the gods would do everything in their power to stop his conquest.

He asked Sambara to call a few pashurivas, the shapeshifting demons who resembled small-sized adults and could transform into small animals or birds. Using them as spies had been very useful in the last war against the gods.

Sambara assembled a team of three pashurivas, who could not only shapeshift but also hide in plain sight. These three were the best of the lot and were almost impossible to detect once they changed form. They were treacherous and knew their way around Bhuloka.

To see how capable they were, Harkasura called the pashurivas into the windowless court he had just created within the ironstone fort. He sat on the throne and watched the three of them appear before him.

"Show me what you've got," Harkasura thundered. As he spoke, Sambara and the pashurivas caught glimpses of fire and smoke coming out through his mouth. Nervous already, they grew more anxious.

The first pashuriva bowed in front of him with folded hands. Next, he raised his hands, turned into a rat and ran around the court. With one giant step, Harkasura stomped on his tail. The pashuriva squeaked loudly. Harkasura picked him up by the tail and tossed him from hand to hand before dropping him back on the ground.

"That was entertaining. What can *you* do?" Harkasura turned his eyes toward the second pashuriva, who turned himself into a small dog. He picked up the puny animal, opened his fire-breathing mouth and threatened to swallow him. After letting the dog squirm for a few moments, he let him go. The frightful experience made him forget how to bark, for a while.

The third pashuriva turned into a raven. Harkasura grabbed the bird in his hands as he tried to fly away and squeezed him tightly. The raven worked hard to get away, but he couldn't escape Harkasura's grasp. He couldn't even caw.

"You are puny little demons," Harkasura said as he let the raven go. "I can crush you whenever I wish. Do you know why I toyed with you just now?"

"No, Lord," all three replied at the same time with their eyes looking down.

"I want you to remember this experience and understand that if you fail to deliver what I ask of you, then no one can save you from my wrath. Now go! Find out what the gods know and what their plan is. Do you understand?"

"Yes, Lord."

"Do you have faith in them?" Harkasura turned to Sambara and questioned.

"Yes, my lord. These are the best pashuriva spies we have in our realm."

"Remember, you puny pipsqueaks. Don't try to act clever. Don't do anything that will draw attention to you."

"Yes, my Lord."

Harkasura raised his trident and tapped it on the floor. Taking that as a sign to leave the court, the three pashurivas shifted into their original shape, and quickly disappeared through the door.

"Once we know what the gods are planning, we can devise our strategy and then march on them with our new, fierce army," Harkasura growled at Sambara, who also quietly left the court.

I see myself

"It is time for us to go search for the Pashupatastra," Narada said at the end of the training on the third evening.

"Are you sure about that? Do you think we are ready?" Advik had his doubts.

"Can you improve your skills? Yes, certainly. Time, however, is not on our side. We have reason to believe Harkasura is resurrected and will soon be on the move."

"But where will we go to find the weapon?" asked Advik.

"That is a good question. What do you all think? Where should we go?"

"I think we should go to Hastinapur, the capital city of the Kauravas and Pandavas. We went with our Ma and Papa a couple of years ago. There are a few temples that are supposed to be from the time of the Mahabharata," Riya offered. "Maybe Vrishaketu thought a temple would be a safe place to hide it?"

"Alright. Let us go to Hastinapur first and hopefully, we will at least find a clue there. We need to get there before Harkasura finds out about us."

"Is he looking for us?" Advik looked concerned.

"Harkasura is smart and shrewd, and I think he will collect all the information he can before leaving Rasatala."

"What kind of information?"

"I am not sure, but if I were him, I would expect the gods to get to the one thing that would finish me forever and find out more about the humans who will help in the process."

"Now that is scary! Why didn't you tell us that before?" Advik asked.

"I didn't want to scare you before you were ready. I think you are prepared to handle any threat that might come your way."

"Can you hide us from the eyes of Harkasura till we find the Pashupatastra?" Samar thought the longer they could hold off the confrontation, the better their chances of victory.

"I can try, but there are no guarantees. You have to watch out for yourselves and not say anything that will give away who you are."

"So what do we do next? How do we go to Hastinapur?" Advik asked.

"How do we leave Meerut without worrying our parents? If the asuras are looking for us, they'll also be in danger, won't they?" Riya worried.

"You are right, Riya," Narada replied. "I don't think it is advisable to go away without telling your parents. Do you think if you own up and tell them you will be fighting the ferocious Harkasura, they will believe you?"

"No, I don't think anyone is going to believe us if we tell the truth," Riya said honestly. "But then what do we do?"

"We can say we are going on a field trip," Samar said brightly. "But then it is summer break... And what will Advik say?" Samar quashed his idea himself.

They tossed ideas around but nothing worked. After a few minutes, they looked back at Narada in despair.

"What if they never found out that you left Meerut?" Narada suggested.

"How is that even possible?" asked Riya.

"Have you heard the story of Maya Sita from the epic Ramayana?" It didn't ring any bells for the children, and Narada couldn't pass up the chance to tell a good story.

"To understand this, we must go back to the days of the fourteen-year exile of Lord Rama, Sita, and Lakshmana. One day, the fire god Agni visited Rama. He had come to warn him about the intentions of the demon king Ravana who was hatching a plan to abduct Sita."

"So Rama knew that Ravana was going to kidnap Sita? Then why didn't he stop him?" Advik asked.

"A good question, Advik. You see, Rama knew that his duty on Bhuloka was to destroy the demon king, and this was how he was going to be able to wage war against Ravana."

"But then why would he let Sita suffer?"

"Exactly, he didn't want her to endure the agony. So he asked Agni how he could do both. Agni told Rama that he could create a maya, an illusion of Sita that was just like her and could fool everyone, including Lakshmana. Rama agreed, and a Maya Sita took Sita's place. She was kept safe until Ravana was defeated, at which time Sita performed the Agni Pariksha. Maya Sita walked into the flames and, Sita emerged, safe and sound." Narada looked around, taking a considerable pause.

"Are you suggesting that we let three mayas take our place, so our parents don't know we're gone?" Riya inferred quickly.

"Now that is very clever. What do you think about that?"

"But we don't know how to do that!" said Advik.

"Well, you leave that to me. But you have to tell me you're fine with that plan."

The kids looked at each other. "I want to see what my maya version looks like." Samar was excited to see what a mirror image of him would be like. They huddled and talked for a minute or so.

"Okay, we agree to the plan," Advik finally told Narada.

"Very good, close your eyes now. Narayan, Narayan!" Narada too closed his eyes, folded his hands and uttered some mantras.

A fire erupted in the room, and three human forms stepped out of the blaze. The children could feel the heat of the fire but didn't dare to open their eyes.

"Open your eyes now," Narada said. The fire disappeared as they did. They couldn't believe what they were seeing. In front of them stood their identical selves!

Samar, who was most excited to see his maya, raised his right hand. The Maya Samar promptly gave him a high-five and Samar looked excitedly at his friends. He was astounded at how life-like his illusion felt. Advik rubbed his eyes and looked once more at his double. Riya was cautiously touching her maya. Before long, all six were laughing and talking to one another.

As the noise level escalated, Narada clapped his hands. All six zipped their lips and looked at Narada. "Now that you've had your fun, the maya versions will hide here while you three get ready. Pack your bags, and the mayas will take your place when we leave tomorrow."

Here we come!

The next morning, when Sanaa and Shiv were getting ready to go to the hospital, Advik said he wasn't feeling too well and asked if he could stay home.

"If you aren't feeling well, we can get you checked at the hospital. Won't that be better?" Sanaa enquired.

"Yes Ma, don't worry about me. I think it is just an upset stomach. You take care of Dada. Maybe I can visit him in the evening." Sanaa tried to convince him, but he wouldn't budge. With the need to get a move on, she and Shiv left, telling Advik to stay quietly in bed.

As soon as the door closed, Advik hopped up from the bed, grabbed his backpack and began packing. He took only a pair of jeans, three shirts, and some undergarments. He wasn't sure how long he'd be gone, but Advik was certain that he would make them last. He didn't want it to be overly evident to his parents that anything was missing, so he kept his packing minimal. He was sure however, to bring the book of mantras that Narada had given him, and his weapons in their compact form.

He heard a knock on the front door and answered it. There stood Riya and Samar, bags packed and smiling brightly.

"Ready?" Advik asked. "Did you pack your weapons?"

"Yeah, we got the sword and the spear. I also borrowed my father's travel toolkit. We may need it. So yes, let's do this," Samar held out his hand and yelled. Riya and Advik placed their palms on his.

"Harkasura, here we come," the three kids said in unison. Next, they folded their hands, closed their eyes and said, "Narayan, Narayan!"

Sure enough, Narada appeared out of thin air wearing jeans and a T-shirt.

"We are ready, let's go," Advik said with strong determination in his voice. "Are you going to zap us directly to Hastinapur and have the mayas take our place?"

"Narayan, Narayan! Unfortunately, I can't transport all of you to Hastinapur. I can go there in an instant, but you have to take local transport," Narada replied.

"You mean, a bus? I have never taken one in India. Is it safe? Can't the gods help us?" Advik was concerned.

"It's not so bad, Advik. Here we are about to save the world, and you are worried about safety on a public bus! We'll take you with us, you American!" Riya said, laughing. Samar laughed too and patted Advik on his back.

"I'm not worried. I just haven't done that before. I don't have any money for the bus, either." Advik tried to save face.

"Come on, don't be mean to Advik. Getting the gods involved may draw attention. So we are better off using the bus. And anyway, I'm coming with you too," Narada added.

"Okay, okay. We have some money from our piggy bank. Let's go find the Pashupatastra then," Riya said with a smile.

Narada closed his eyes and uttered "Narayan, Narayan!" The next moment the three mayas appeared. The kids were again awestruck. They started giving instructions to their likenesses. But they were interrupted and hurried out of the house by Narada.

As they walked to the nearest bus station, the cow incident replayed in Advik's mind. He walked carefully to avoid stepping on anything unfamiliar on the road. Riya and Samar giggled at his jumpy walk. Narada smiled quietly.

Advik knew he was making a spectacle of himself, but couldn't help it. Walking on the streets in India was all new to him. After several minutes, they noticed a stray dog following several yards behind them and Narada grew nervous.

"What's the matter? Are you scared of dogs?"

Narada looked at Advik, walked fast to the front of the group and then replied, "I don't like dogs; one bit me several centuries ago, and I haven't liked them since."

"But you are the messenger of the gods, how come you are afraid?"

"I'm immortal, not immune to pain. Since I can remember everything from the beginning of time, I never get to forget the pain of things that have happened to me," Narada replied, his pace quickening.

The kids laughed at his response but helped Narada by shielding him from it. Samar, looking to solve the problem, pretended to throw something at the dog. With its tail between its legs, it took off running.

As they reached the messy and bustling bus station, Advik tried to take it all in. Overflowing buses pulled in and unloaded crowds of people, more crowds rushed in to take their seats.

All around them was confusion and noise. It seemed that everyone was shouting at one another, while garbled announcements came over the loudspeaker. Advik spoke very little Hindi, but doubted he would have understood the announcements even if he spoke it.

Riya and Samar dragged Advik towards the bus to Hastinapur. Advik breathed a sigh of relief when he saw that their bus was nowhere near as crowded as many of the others.

They climbed inside and took their seats. Advik and Riya sat together, and Samar and Narada took the seats directly behind them. Moments later, they were on their way.

Advik placed a hand on his chest to feel the racing beat of his heart. Riya smiled at him reassuringly.

"I'm scared," Advik replied.

"You aren't alone, Advik. We'll take care of this together."

Samar overheard the conversation and got up from his seat.

"Let's bring Harkasura down!" He was pumped up. Narada looked at him and put his fingers to his lips.

"Quiet! We don't want to draw any attention."

"Oh yes, I forgot. I'm sorry." Samar slipped back in his seat.

Little did they know that even now, at the very beginning of their journey, they were already too late.

Book of mantras

Hastinapur, compared to Meerut, was a relatively small town. As they arrived, the passengers grabbed their belongings and made a mad dash for the door. Advik was taken aback by the sudden rush of activity. "Everyone here is always in a hurry," said Riya. "Come on, grab your backpack and let's go."

As they walked out of the main entrance of the bus station, a crowd of ricksha drivers gathered around, asking where they wanted to go. Advik, reeling from the chaos, was dragged along by Riya and Samar, who were more than comfortable dealing with the commotion. Narada followed them serenely.

"So where do we go first?" Advik asked.

"Well, that is a good question," Narada replied. "I believe we should head to the Pandeshwar Temple."

"Oh! I remember that one. It is the Shiva temple where the Pandavas used to pray and still has the idol from that time," Riya jumped in with an excited voice.

"Yes, that's right. By the way, you should know that Vrishaketu broke the Pashupatastra into three small arrows and we need to find all of them, along with the mantra, to invoke the weapon."

"So we are on a treasure hunt to find three arrows and a mantra. But we don't know where to begin." Advik was concerned again.

"To invoke the astra, Advik needs to fire off three arrows together with the mantra?" Samar had his doubts as well.

"Yes, that's right," Narada said again.

"What is the role of the gods in this? What are they doing to help? We're only children, and we have left everything behind to help them." It was Riya's turn to voice her anxiety.

"The gods will help in their own way. You must remember that you are all here because they need to defeat Harkasura. They've sent me to help you along, and the only thing I'm certain of is that you can defeat him."

"How can you be so sure about that?"

"I'm going with my gut." Narada smiled. "My intuition has a hundred percent record for being correct. Since that covers the last several thousand years, I see no reason to doubt it now." He looked proud of himself.

Suddenly, Narada spun round to see a small dog wagging its tail and barking happily at him. The smile left his face as fear overtook him and he began to run. Eager for a game of chase, the dog joyfully followed, barking all the while. The children doubled over in laughter, as the messenger of the gods fled the tiny ball of fluff and climbed the nearest tree.

"We should rescue Naradamuni," Riya said, trying to stifle her laughter, with a palm clamped over her face, while the boys rushed to Narada's rescue.

When the dog saw the boys running towards him, he stopped barking and ran away. The relief on Narada's face was short-lived as they heard the harsh call of a very large raven overhead. The bird swooped down on the tree, grabbed Narada in its beak and vanished into the sky.

Shell-shocked by what had just happened before their eyes, the children looked at one another, unable to say a word. They were suddenly all alone in a strange city, and the one and only person they were relying on, in this scary adventure, was gone! Samar finally broke the silence.

"Did you all see what I just saw?"

"How could a raven lift a grown man and fly away like that?" Advik was still not sure what had just happened. "How is it even possible?"

"I don't think there's any doubt about what we saw. I don't know how that happened, but Naradamuni isn't coming back on his own," Riya added.

"But he can teleport himself back, can't he?" Advik was cautious.

"Could this have something to do with Harkasura? If it does, then Naradamuni's powers may not work. Give it a shot, try to summon him." Advik put his hands together and closed his eyes, hoping against hope that Narada would return.

"Narayan, Narayan!" Advik opened his eyes and looked around. To everyone's disappointment, Narada did not appear. "Oh no!" Riya said, disappointed.

"So what do we do now?" Advik started getting nervous. "Should we go back to Meerut?"

"But the gods sent us on this mission. To turn back now would be pointless. We can do this, Advik. Also remember, Naradamuni said he believed we were ready," Samar tried to breathe some hope into him.

"Without Naradamuni? How can we find the Pashupatastra without his help?"

"We can at least try." Samar was not ready to give up. Both the boys looked at Riya.

She took a big breath and replied, "I have to agree with Samar. We're running out of time, and the gods may be able to send more help later on. For now, we need to keep to the plan and keep moving."

"Yes, exactly. Let's go to the Pandeshwar Temple and look for the first clue," Samar added. Advik wasn't convinced, but he was out-voted. He did see their point of view, but it didn't change how he felt.

He closed his eyes, opened his backpack, and reached for the book of mantras.

"What are you doing?" Samar questioned.

Advik untied the orange cloth to reveal an ancient book. Samar and Riya looked anxiously at the picture of the sun on the cover, as he randomly turned to a page.

"Riya, can you read what it says?"

ॐ नमो अग्नि देवाय नमः।
मम शत्रुंज्वालय नाशय हुं फट्।।

Om namo Agni devaaya namah.
Mama shatrunjvaalaya, naashaya hum fatt.

Riya read out the mantra slowly, trying her best at reading Sanskrit. It was the Agni Astramantra. Riya and Samar looked at Advik. He felt reassured for some reason and said, "Let's go to the Pandeshwar temple," as he stashed the book in his backpack.

"Now you're talking," Riya and Samar said, as they started walking.

The temple

After asking for directions, Advik, Samar and Riya walked down an unpaved path shaded by trees, among old ruins. Advik began to have doubts as to whether he had made the right choice, when they spotted the temple.

A dusty orange-coloured arch with two wrought iron gates was the main entrance.

"Shri Pracheen Pandeshwar Mahadev Temple," Samar read the writing on the arch. "We've reached the right place. Now what?"

"Let's go inside and see if we can find any clues."

The three entered and looked around. A giant banyan tree stood just outside the entrance to the temple.

"This tree has been here for the last 7000 years," the kids overheard someone say. Walking up to it they looked hard for any clues on the tree trunk, whispering to each other about what might be a sign. After spending quite some time, they couldn't get any leads, so they decided to give up and enter the temple.

Climbing up a couple of stairs, they entered the small sanctum that housed the Shivling. Riya and Samar folded their hands, Advik quickly did the same, and they began looking around. Major renovations had been done a few years ago, with new porcelain tiles added to the walls. All traces of clues would surely have been destroyed. Samar tried to touch the Linga to see if there was anything there.

"Hey, you! Move away from the Linga. Don't touch it with your dirty hands," someone shouted out.

Samar stepped back, and everyone looked in the direction of the voice. The priest of the temple, a frail, angry, old man with bright eyes, a white beard and orange robes, came running inside. To Advik he seemed to be as old as the temple!

The priest started yelling at the kids. The sandalwood tilak on his forehead moved as he raised his eyebrows, and Advik thought that it looked like Lord Shiva's third eye that was about to open and destroy everything around it. Riya and Samar were scared too, but then Riya found the courage to speak up.

"Please don't yell at us. We are doing the work of the gods, and if you don't let us carry on, the world will end."

"What do you mean, the work of the gods? Have you kids gone crazy?" The priest thought that they were out to create some trouble.

"Panditji, you will not understand. Please let us look around. We aren't here to do anything wrong. This work is urgent. Please," Samar said earnestly.

The priest looked into their eyes. They appeared to be genuine and sincere, so he calmed down, took a deep breath and said, "I don't know why, but I believe you. Tell me what you are really up to and why you are here. My name is Pandit Ramashankar, and I have been the priest of this temple for the last thirty years. Members of our family have been the priests here for the last four hundred years.

If there is anyone who knows enough about this temple to be able to help you, it would be me."

"Can we sit down somewhere private and talk?" Advik was concerned that someone might overhear them, and he wasn't sure how the priest would react to what they were about to tell him.

"Okay, come with me," Ramashankar said. He led them to a small room at the back of the temple with one window, a ceiling fan and four chairs.

"Now tell me what is going on," he said. A thought crossed his mind that the three were runaways. But he was a wise man and he chose to listen first. The kids collapsed into the chairs. "Advik, why don't you start? If there is any problem with understanding your accent, I can fill Panditji in," said Riya. Advik nodded and started, not missing anything out.

Fifteen minutes later, Ramashankar sat in total disbelief. He knew the ancient stories they mentioned and was reminded of his childhood when he'd heard them. Still, all this was hard for him to believe. Where was the catch?

"Hmm... I am still not sure."

"Advik, the book! Show him the book Naradamuni gave you!" Riya interrupted excitedly.

"Oh yes!" Advik pulled the book out of his backpack and handed it to Ramashankar. The priest couldn't believe his eyes. He read the Sanskrit inscription and realised that it was no ordinary book. He turned the pages carefully, admiring the thin metal. There was no way this book was created recently. Scratching his head, he looked from the book to the children.

"Let's say I believe you… Why do you think you will find any clues here in the temple?"

"Vrishaketu must have hidden the clues and the mantra in a place that he believed would be safe. Given that he lived in these parts and this was a small temple that wouldn't attract too much attention, he probably decided to keep them here. We think it makes sense to start here," Advik replied.

"When you were telling me the background, I remembered something from my childhood."

"What is it?" the three asked in excited voices.

"I must have been around ten years old. I was sleeping in my bed in our ancestral house, which is close to the temple, and woke up with a bad dream. I spotted my father, who was the priest then, leaving through the front door. I got curious and decided to follow him."

"In the middle of the night, you were following him?" Advik asked, hanging on to his every word.

"Yes. I wasn't sure what my father was doing so late, so I decided to tail him. I kept a safe distance to ensure he didn't know I was behind him. He came here to the temple and stood outside the inner sanctum for a few seconds, with folded hands."

The kids listened attentively.

"Then, he walked to the banyan tree and circled it three times, stopping halfway through each circle to stomp on the ground. When he finished his rotations, the ground opened up to a secret door. He walked to the door and disappeared. I was not brave enough to follow him, so I stayed outside and saw the ground return to normal. There was no evidence of a door ever having been there. I ran away, frightened, and got back into bed."

"You didn't find out what was under the secret door?" Advik was his curious self again.

"When I saw him the next day, I asked him about what I saw that night. He said it was probably just a dream and changed the subject."

"So he never told you about it, even later on in life?"

"No, I somehow convinced myself that it was a dream like my father said. My father later died in a sudden accident, so if he had planned to tell me, he missed his chance. He did, however, leave me a notebook with a drawing in it. Come to think of it, it might just have the answer to opening that very door."

"How has no one else found out about this?"

"You children spent some time circling the tree earlier, but did you notice anything?" All three shook their heads. "It is very well-hidden. If no one was meant to know but those entrusted to guard the temple, it makes sense that no one has found it. Had I not heard your story, I too would never have thought about it."

"Can you show us the book and guide us to the secret door?"

"We can't do it now. There are too many people in the temple," Samar added.

"You are right. We have to wait until night. We'll come back then and try to open it."

"What do we do until then?" Advik was worried.

"My home is not far from here. I can take you there to get something to eat; you can play with my five-year-old granddaughter and, when it's time, we'll come back."

"Your son must be a priest too? Where is he?"

"He is, but he is not in town today. He has gone to Meerut. He will come back the day after tomorrow."

The kids went into a huddle and talked about the plan. A couple of minutes later, Riya said, "Thank you very much, Panditji. We will do as you say." Ramashankar smiled and put his wrinkled palm on her head. They left the temple and headed to his home, feeling a lot better than they had felt since the raven attack in the morning.

The first riddle

The children had a fun evening, spending time with Ramashankar's family, eating delicious homemade food, and playing games. Ramashankar had told his daughter-in-law that they were the children of a fellow priest, visiting for the night. Advik, however, not being able to eat rice with his fingers comfortably, could have raised some suspicion, but everyone had a big laugh as Advik made an absolute mess of his plate. The rice slipped through his fingers and was splattered all around his mouth. When he had finished eating, it looked as though he had gone to war with his food. Ramashankar's granddaughter cackled at the spectacle and rolled on the floor.

Advik, never one to appreciate laughter at his expense, vowed never to eat rice in India again. Ramashankar, noticing his souring mood, ruffled Advik's hair and told him not to worry about it.

The priest's house was old and similar in style to Advik's grandfather's. It had an open courtyard in the middle and a row of rooms bordering it. A tulsi plant stood right in the centre of the courtyard.

After dinner, when his family was busy, Ramashankar called the three children to his room, which was to the left of the courtyard. He was holding his father's worn-out notebook in one hand and flipped through the pages with the other. He showed them the book and pointed to a diagram. It was a spiral with a simple sketch of a tree in the middle. There were six markings on the spiral, three on the left and three on the right side. On the left of the spiral was a drawing of the sun. There was some writing under it, which looked like a shloka.

"What does the writing under the drawing say?" Advik was curious.

"It reads '*Gyansiddhi satve bhavati n itarai janai*'. It roughly translates to 'Those who deserve will find their way, others will not.' I think my father somehow knew that he wasn't going to be able to show me the secret door, so he drew this so I could help when needed."

"That's pretty cryptic," Riya hummed as she stared at the drawing. "Oh wait! I get it. These markings here must be the places where your father was stomping when circling the tree." Excitement filled her voice. "And the Sun shows the East. It is the direction of the rising sun, who is considered to be the father of Karna and the grandfather of Vrishaketu."

"I think so too," Ramashankar agreed.

"Does that mean we know how to open the secret hatch?" asked Advik.

"If there is any truth in this diagram, then yes."

"But we still don't know if we will find anything useful in there."

"Yes, but a secret chamber in the temple grounds seems like a logical place to start, wouldn't you agree?" The very idea excited Samar.

The others agreed and decided to meet at 11:30 p.m near the tulsi plant. Ramashankar made arrangements for the children to sleep in one of the rooms. None of them could even think of sleeping, but they decided to try and get some rest before their mission.

Time seemed to drag as they lay in their beds with their eyes wide open, listening to the sounds of the town die down slowly. Each wondered about how their mayas were doing, whether their parents had noticed anything different, and if their secret was going to be exposed.

Finally, it was time to leave. The children tiptoed their way to the courtyard and waited for Ramashankar. He came there with a bag.

"I got some torches and some water."

"Okay. Let's go, then." Samar couldn't hide his eagerness as they slowly walked out of the house. Ramashankar handed the torches to everyone. "Advik, why don't you lead the way? Samar and Riya, you can follow him, and I will light the way from behind."

"No, why don't you come up front? I am a bit scared. Plus, you know the way," Advik responded.

"Don't worry Advik, nothing will happen. If you want, I can be in front," Riya assured the group. Advik just nodded his head.

The path to the temple was surrounded by trees that gently swayed in the night breeze. Their shadows gave a creepy air to their journey, making Advik nervous. He laughed off the feeling that they would spring to life and grab him.

Riya opened the gate of the temple and everyone rushed to the banyan tree. Ramashankar opened the notebook again.

"I think we should start here," he said, looking at the diagram again, and walked to the east of the tree. "The first marking must be here somewhere." No one questioned him, as he was easily the best authority they had on this subject.

Ramashankar and the kids stopped at the rough spot closest to the east of tree as per the diagram in the notebook, and stomped the ground. They carefully followed the circular pattern around the tree.

As they got close to the final mark on the outermost spiral, everyone could feel their hearts racing at full speed. They all jumped on the last spot and looked around waiting for the secret hatch to open. But nothing happened.

They exchanged anxious looks and saw great disappointment in each other's eyes. "Why don't we try stomping on the last spot again?" Ramashankar said.

"Are you sure?" Advik questioned. "Don't you think we should spread out a little and stomp at all the markings so that we cover all possible spots?"

"No, I don't think it is going to work that way. There must be something else," Riya chimed in with her eyes lost in deep thought. "But what could it be?" Samar was out of ideas. Suddenly a thought struck Riya's mind like a bolt. "I think the markings on the spiral have something to do with the sun."

"How do they relate to the sun? Oh, wait! Is it possible that these markings show the direction of sunrise and sunset?" Advik had an epiphany.

"You are right, Advik," Ramashankar replied. "The Sun rises a little bit in the northeast in midwinter and sets in the northwest. The opposite happens in midsummer. We call winter solstice Uttarayana and summer solstice Dakshinayana. If we go with your logic, then the sun rises at 28 degrees southeast and sets at 28 degrees northeast on Uttarayaana. On Dakshinayana, the Sun rises at 28 degrees northeast and sets 28 degrees northwest."

"So we need to stomp on the spiral at the 28 degrees. Is that what we are concluding here?" Samar added, "but how do we determine the exact degree?"

"We will have to do some approximation. We start with a 45 degree angle and then do half of that and walk in the opposite direction," Riya said as she walked to the east side of the tree. Before anyone could figure out what she meant, she yelled, "I think here should be the first marking."

"Perhaps it is worth a shot," Ramashankar added as he, Advik and Samar followed Riya. Everyone looked at the diagram again, spread out a little and stomped on the first spot. They grew anxious as they traversed the spiral path once more, following Riya's lead, and stomped on the ground on the spots she picked.

Advik felt as though his heart was ready to pop out of his chest. His friends seemed to have the same look on their faces as they approached the sixth marker. Even in the brisk night air, they all began to sweat.

They got to the last marker and took a big, deep breath, stomped on the ground and waited anxiously. A few seconds passed and nothing happened. Advik covered his face with his hands in disappointment.

Clang... clang... a loud metal on metal noise pierced from the east through the quiet and the ground shook under their feet. Samar and Advik fell because of the movement and looked startled. Riya looked shaken too. Ramashankar pulled the boys up, and all of them rushed to the east of the tree.

A two-foot hole appeared where they had stood a moment ago. They had managed to open the secret door.

Can't solve this one

"Are you sure nothing lives down there in that hole?" Advik asked.

"I have no idea. I never saw anything come out that night," Ramashankar replied taking a deep breath. "We have to go down to find out."

The children nodded, scared but determined. Ramashankar shone a torch down, and they could see a very dark chamber with some stone steps leading into it. Advik craned his neck to see where they were headed, but it was of no use.

"I can't see where the stairs are going. I wish we had Naradamuni with us. He could have helped more."

"I agree, but we have to do without him. Why don't we go down and find out," Riya replied. "We need to do everything we can to find the Pashupatastra."

"For a change, I don't have a different opinion here," Samar added, as he jumped onto the first stone step that led down to the chamber.

"Be careful, don't do anything stupid," Riya cautioned him. She, Advik and Ramashankar climbed down behind him.

"I've made it to the bottom of the steps," Samar yelled from only about ten steps down. "There's nothing to worry about, just step carefully." He wielded his small torch like a sword. The darkness was overpowering and seemed to swallow up what little light it provided.

Once Ramashankar too had made it to the bottom, lights from their four torches did only slightly more than one to light the passage that lay before them at the bottom of the stairs.

"Let's go through," Samar's voice was excited once more. "But let's walk with our backs touching, so we face all directions."

"Good idea," Ramashankar said. He was amazed that the kids were acting so brave when he was feeling scared. With their backs against each other, they started walking down the passage filled with crawling insects and spider webs. It certainly looked like no one had set foot in there for ages.

The passage led to a small chamber. It was probably six feet long, four feet wide and six feet tall. The four of them filled the room. It was dark and very quiet. They could hear each other breathing. There was a small raised platform in the middle of the room. There was nothing else besides it.

"It doesn't make sense. Why would someone build this elaborate structure and not have anything inside?" Advik was puzzled.

"Maybe someone removed whatever was here before we came."

"But who would do that? No one knows about this place." Ramashankar was sure.

"Maybe your father removed it," Riya said, with hesitation.

"I don't think so. If my father did that, he would have told me, or at least mentioned something in the notebook," Ramashankar said, flipping the pages of his father's notebook.

"If that is the case, then I think whatever was here is still here. Maybe we need to look carefully." Advik forced himself to be optimistic. "Let's search every inch of this chamber before we quit."

"Advik you take the back wall, Riya and Samar you can search the side walls, and I will search the rest of the room," Ramashankar said.

"Okay, Panditji," the kids replied and began their assigned jobs. With the help of the torch, they slowly touched every inch of the room. After fifteen minutes they came up empty-handed.

"Doesn't look like we are meant to find whatever it was," Riya said with frustration.

"I just don't get it. All this trouble for nothing? How am I going to find the way to defeat Harkasura?" Advik said with anger and slammed his fist on the altar.

Suddenly, with a whirring noise, the top of the platform split into two. It was so unexpected that it left them dumbfounded. Advik peered closer. Inside the hollow platform was a stone tablet with some inscriptions on it.

"I think I've found it! I've found the mantra!" Advik screamed, picking up the tablet and raising his palm. He felt as if a bolt of lightning had passed through his body. Samar excitedly gave him a high-five. Advik's face was shining. He looked at the tablet again. "But I can't read this. How am I going to invoke the weapon?"

"Well, we have Panditji. He can help us," Riya said. Advik nodded and handed over the tablet to Ramashankar. He blew air on the tablet and got rid of the dust to read the inscriptions.

किमिच्छति नर:काश्याम्?
भूपानां को रणे हितः?
कोवन्द्यःसर्व देवानाम्?
दीयताम् एकम् उत्तरम्।।

Kimichchati narahaKaashyaam?
Bhoopaanaam ko raney hitaha?
Kovandyahasarva devaanaam?
Deeyataam ekam uttaram.

"That is the mantra for the Pashupatastra?" Samar was eager to know.

"Shush...," Riya tried to keep him quiet. "Is that correct Panditji?"

"I am afraid, but it appears that we don't have the mantra for the invocation of the Pashupatastra. But from what I read here, it looks like this is some sort of a riddle."

"Riddle? Really? After all this, we still aren't close to finding the mantra?" Advik was not happy.

"Can you describe the riddle?" Riya asked.

"It says: 'What does a man want in Kashi? What does a king wish for in a war? Who commands the respect of all the gods? Give me an answer'."

"Is that it? What does it mean?" Samar almost yelled. Ramashankar looked thoughtful. "I'm not sure. Maybe it is a clue to something, maybe it isn't."

"What should we do? We're back to square one. I really miss Naradamuni now. I wonder how he is doing? Whether he has been harmed in any way." Riya sounded concerned.

As Advik ran his fingers along the surface of the tablet, he felt something change within him. It was almost as if the tablet was telling him that this was not the end but just the beginning. He thought of his grandfather and new-found energy began to flow through him.

"Okay, this is a minor setback, but we can do this. We can keep going! I am sure we will find Naradamuni and he will be okay." He spoke with such conviction that Riya and Samar stared at him. He sounded so different from his usual, sceptical self.

Ramashankar was observing the tablet closely. "I think there is more to this tablet," he said quietly. "Can you see there are three holes in this corner?"

Advik, Samar, and Riya looked carefully at the corner he was pointing at and realised that there were indeed three holes.

"Don't these look like keyholes to you?" Samar asked. "But for what sort of keys?"

"I think we need to solve the riddle and that will lead us to the keys," Advik suggested.

"You are right, Advik, I was thinking the same," Riya added. "But that means there is something else that is hidden in this tablet."

"Maybe the mantra! Once we get that, we can defeat Harkasura," Samar yelled, pumping his right fist in the air. "Oh wait, you guys, remember Naradamuni told us that Vrishaketu divided the astra into three arrows. Maybe the riddle leads to three arrows and together they open the tablet?"

"It is good to see that you are building on each other's ideas," Ramashankar spoke up. "But I think it is very late to do anything further right now. Let us go home with the tablet, and we can solve the riddle in the morning. Just thinking about it isn't going to help right now."

"But I can't sleep now," Advik complained.

"Neither can we," Samar and Riya said together.

"If we don't get back, someone may come to visit the temple early in the morning and see us here," Ramashankar warned. The kids reluctantly agreed to wrap up.

They climbed out of the chamber with the tablet and stomped on the first marker. With the same grating sound, the hole in the ground closed and became impossibly even again.

Advik clutched the tablet to his chest, thinking only of the riddle as they made their way back to Ramashankar's home.

'What does a man want in Kashi? What does a king wish for in a war? Who commands the respect of all the gods? Give me an answer.'

Four heads together

Back in Ramashankar's home, the children took their weary bodies to bed. They lay in their room, tired but not ready for sleep. Also, they were by now missing their homes and families. Not wanting to let go of the tablet, Advik slipped it under his pillow and drifted into a restless sleep filled with dreams of solving the riddle.

Advik was being jostled awake. "Just one more minute," he mumbled sleepily as he always did. Then hearing laughter around him, he jumped up to find Ramashankar's granddaughter tugging on his blanket.

The first thing he did was to check under his pillow to see if the tablet was just where he'd left it. He ran his fingers over the inscription once more, hoping that enlightenment would strike him suddenly with the answer to the riddle. He checked for his backpack and the book of mantras next.

Samar and Riya were smiling at him. "We were wondering when you were going to get up, sleepy head. The two of us hardly slept. Kept thinking about the riddle," Riya chirped.

"I think I was dreaming about it but couldn't solve it." Advik smiled.

"I don't think you can solve it anyway. It's not the Da Vinci Code, my American friend," Samar laughed. "We all need to put our heads together and figure out the answer."

"Yup! Give me twenty minutes."

"Twenty? What are you going to do for that long? Put on make-up?" Samar roared with laughter.

"Come on, Samar. Let the poor guy do whatever he needs to. In the meantime, why don't you play with this little girl?" Riya pointed at Ramashankar's granddaughter, who smiled brightly at her guests.

"No, I don't want to play with little girls. You should do it."

"Oh, I get it now. You would rather spend your time thinking about me putting on make-up," Advik shot back and raced off to get ready.

After a late breakfast of hot parathas, which they gulped down as fast as they could, they rushed back to the tablet. Ramashankar was back from the morning rituals over at the temple, and he joined them.

"Any more ideas?" asked Riya.

"What is Kashi?" Advik wondered, puzzled.

"Varanasi! You didn't know that?" Samar scoffed.

"Samar, there is no reason to act smart right now," Riya cautioned him.

"Oh, I didn't know that," Advik said sheepishly. "But you don't know what the Windy City is, so you can't blame me."

"You mean Chicago?" Samar replied with a smirk on his face. "I know about your country, you know."

Advik was stumped, but he didn't give up. "Can you tell me what the Big Easy is?"

It was Samar's turn to get baffled. He just smiled back and jerked his shoulders.

"Aha! It's New Orleans," Advik said and waved his hands in the air.

"Now, we can start working on the riddle if you guys are done," Riya stepped in. "Don't people go to Varanasi to die, so they go straight to Swargaloka?" she asked.

"You are right, Riya," Ramashankar replied. "काश्याम्मरणम्मुक्ति।। (KashyaamMaranamMukti). It means, 'Death in Kashi is liberation'."

"In that case, I think the answer to the first question in the riddle is 'death'," Advik said, with eyes sparkling. Then he realised what he'd said and gulped.

"I think you are right, Advik," Ramashankar said softly.

"And the second question: What does a king wish for in a war? Isn't the answer 'victory'?" Samar had his moment in the sun!

"Death and Victory, what does it mean?" Advik said as he scratched his head. "Also who commands the respect of all the gods? I can't make sense of the answers we came up with." Samar shook his head.

"Maybe we're doing it the wrong way," Riya said.

"What do you mean?" Advik questioned.

"Shouldn't the answers be in Sanskrit?" Riya replied, looking at Ramashankar.

"That is what I was thinking too," the priest agreed. "The word for death in Sanskrit is मृत्यु (mrityu) and, the word for victory is जय (jaya)."

"Together we get मृत्युजय (mrityujaya). Oh, I get it. Isn't Mrityunjaya (मृत्युंजय) another name for Lord Shiva?" Riya was super excited. "And wouldn't he command the respect of all the gods?"

Samar and Advik were stunned. Riya had indeed solved the riddle.

Gibberish?

"So what is the link between Lord Shiva and the clue?" Advik busted the bubble of euphoria with a hard question.

"I think something related to Lord Shiva holds the key to this tablet," Samar replied, "But I don't know what."

"One thing is for sure: whatever it is, it must be something that survived all these years from the time of the Mahabharata," Riya tried to push them to think.

"The only such place we know is the Pandeshwar Temple," Samar said, eyes lighting up.

"But we checked the temple ourselves. Also, why would Vrishaketu hide the first key in the same place as the tablet? That doesn't make sense. I wonder where that raven took Naradamuni. We hadn't counted on doing all this on our own," Advik said dejectedly as the enthusiasm from last night had faded.

"Advik, we all agree with that. But for now, I think we have a clue to something obvious. One thing we didn't check in the temple was the Shivlinga itself." Riya looked at Ramashankar.

"Panditji, do you think that is possible?" Advik asked, trying to hold in his excitement.

"Now that you mentioned it, I have always wondered why there was a notch in the middle of the second line of the Tripundra," the priest replied thoughtfully. "Tripundra is a tilak with three horizontal lines on the forehead," he explained, seeing the confused faces of the children. "You always see it on Lord Shiva's idol and sometimes on the Shivlinga. Each line means something different, but the easiest one to remember is that each line represents a syllable of ॐ (Aum)."

"So the second line represents the sound 'u' of Aum." Advik was quick to conclude.

"Precisely! Now I think there is a notch in the middle of the second line. I always thought that since the Shivlinga is so old, the stone got damaged. But there may be another explanation."

"We should go to the temple right away then." Samar was excited.

Ramashankar nodded. "The inner sanctum is closed, but I will have to open shortly, so it is a good time to go right now."

Samar and Riya leaped to wear their shoes, while Advik packed the tablet in his backpack. They all checked to make sure their weapons were also in their backpacks.

They were on their way in a couple of minutes. No one talked, but everyone was hopeful that the clue they had just deciphered was going to lead to a discovery in the place that Ramashankar had told them about.

As they got close to the temple, their feet picked up speed and their heartbeats accelerated.

"Slow down, or the devotees inside will think something is wrong," Ramashankar advised, as the orange brick walls of the temple came into view. The children slowed their pace as they made their way through the gate, past the few devotees still there and to the inner sanctum, which was closed.

The three children practically jumped into the inner sanctum, and Ramashankar carefully closed the door. The small room plunged into darkness. A lone oil lamp did its best to give some light.

Ramashankar was chanting something in a calm voice, and it felt beautiful listening to it in that quiet darkness, so close to the ancient Shivlinga.

"Please close your eyes and hold out your hands," the priest said as he picked up a small vessel filled with water, and poured the water on the children's palms. "Okay, now switch on your torches."

Advik and Samar shone the torches on the Shivlinga, looking carefully at the second line of the Tripundra. There was indeed a notch in the middle of the centre line. Advik slowly extended his hand and touched the groove.

"I feel something. There is something stuck in here." Everyone in the room got excited.

"Let me see." Samar wanted in on the action.

"Wait, let me see if I can pull it out," Advik replied. "Give me more light." Advik tried to pull out whatever was stuck in there. "It is hard to get hold of, Riya. You have longer nails than me, maybe you can try." Riya too tried to get it out but couldn't.

"The multi-tool set I borrowed from Papa has a pair of tweezers, maybe that will help!" Samar took it out and gently inserted it into the groove. The others held their breath in anticipation. As he tugged, a few orange feathers appeared, attached to a slim bronze shaft. With a faint sound of metal scraping stone, a diamond-shaped head at the other end of the shaft came into view. They stood stunned watching it gleam in the pale light.

"It's an arrow!" Advik said in a hushed voice, his heart pounding.

"And it's got something etched on it! It's so beautiful, and I'm sure it's just as deadly," Samar whispered, feeling pleased about having extracted it. He passed it to Advik, who quickly pulled out the tablet. He inserted the head of the arrow into the first slot. All eyes were fixed on him as he rotated the arrow clockwise, like a key.

Click! A sound of turning gears pierced the quiet as the arrow turned, and a metal piece fell on the ground from inside the tablet. Advik picked it up and stared at the inscription on it.

"What does it say?" Riya asked.

"I don't know. It looks like gibberish to me. It's the same letter repeated over and over," Advik replied as he flipped the piece to see if it revealed anything else. He removed the arrow from the hole and put it in the backpack.

"Panditji?" Riya looked at Ramashankar. Advik handed the piece to him. Ramashankar stared at the piece in the light of the oil lamp and said, "I am not sure what it means, but I think it is probably the second clue."

Wind riders

भूरिभिर्भारिभिर्भीराभू भारैरभिरेभिरे ।
भेरिरेभिभिरभ्राभैरभीरुभिरिभैरिभाः ।।

bhuribhirbhaaribhirbhiraabhu bhaarairabhirebhire.
bherirebhibhirabhraabhairabhirubhiribhairibhaah.

It didn't make any sense to them, even to Ramashankar.

After several moments of trying to reason it out, they heard sounds from outside.

"It's time for the doors to open for puja again. I think you three best go back to the house so that I can let the devotees in. I will meet you there later." The children nodded. They packed the arrow and tablet in Advik's backpack, along with the book of mantras and left the sanctum quickly.

As they walked down the unpaved road to Ramashankar's home, they heard a sound that had been replaying in their minds since the previous day — the raucous cawing of a raven. There was no mistaking what it was.

Samar pulled the other two into a clump of bushes. "Guys, Harkasura's spy is back. It looks like the same raven that lifted Naradamuni."

Peering through the bushes, they could see it sitting on a tree, moving its neck, looking for something. They crowded closer together, feeling one another's breath. Advik kept a firm hand on his backpack as he watched the bird on its perch.

After a few minutes, it seemed to be satisfied that there was nothing to report. With a loud cry, it went gliding into the eastern sky.

"Come on! Let's chase the raven, maybe it'll lead us to Naradamuni!" Caught up in the adventure of the moment, none of them stopped to think about how they would chase a flying bird. They sped down the path to follow their guide's kidnapper. They remained cautious, using the dense green foliage to hide along the way, keeping out of its sight.

With their eyes on the sky, they were suddenly stopped short by a wire fence. The sign on it warned that the area was under the surveillance of the Department of Forests.

"Oh, wait!" said Riya. "This must be where the Pandava's palace used to be — near the Pandeshwar Temple. Some ruins are still there; that's why it's a protected area."

"Should we go in if it's out of bounds?" Advik asked.

"Of course, didn't you see that raven fly right over this fence. I think Naradamuni is just through here. Don't you want to find him or do you think we don't need him anymore?" Samar asked, sharply.

"We do! I was just —" Advik couldn't find the right words.

"If we don't move fast we're going to lose the raven," Riya interrupted, pulling the metal wires apart and scrambling through. Advik and Samar followed.

"Shouldn't we check for a mantra in the book that will help us catch up with the raven?" Samar asked Advik.

"Good idea, Samar." Advik opened his backpack even as they ran and pulled out the book and tossed it to Riya.

"Something that will give us the speed of the wind. Something to do with Lord Vayu?" Samar continued.

"Let me see." Riya's voice was stressed as she turned the pages. A few pages later she yelled, "Here you go. I found it!"

ॐ सर्व प्राणय विद्महे।
तन्नोवायुः प्रचोदयात्।।

Om Sarva praanaya vidhmahe.
tannovaayuh prachodayaath.

Advik quickly memorised it, and they all chanted it together with great concentration. From nowhere, a strong gust of wind appeared and swept them off their feet, and they were in the air following the raven.

"Here, let's hold hands tight, so we stay together," Samar yelled, a little nervous.

It was a weird feeling, not to have the ground under their feet. Advik felt like he was in a convertible, going at top speed on an expressway. "This is so cool!" he shouted excitedly. But then he felt a pit in his stomach. "Wait, what if we can't get back down on the ground!"

"Excellent question, Advik. I wish I had the answer!" Riya tried to appear poised. "Maybe the gods will send us help!" She hoped she was right.

They hurtled toward the raven, who finally swooped down to sit on a tree next to a massive black rock with a deep hollow in it. Sensing the fast-moving cloud, the raven turned. The children knew he had seen them.

Calling out loudly, the raven disappeared into the black rock. The wind dropped the children safely just beside it. "It looks like a cave," Samar finally said. "Do you think Naradamuni is inside?"

"Possibly. But how do we know what else is in the cave?" Riya said cautiously. "Hey, that dog that chased Naradamuni up the tree... what if it was also Harkasura's spy and working with the raven?"

"Oh yes! I forgot about the dog. I'll bet that one dog alone could keep Naradamuni trapped in this cave." Advik nodded his head in agreement.

"Look!" Samar screamed, pointing. Advik and Riya spun around to see three pairs of red-hot eyes staring back at them from the darkness of the cave.

Battling the pashurivas

The children stood terrified as the blazing eyes advanced toward them. But this was just the kind of moment that Narada had trained them to face. Almost without realising it, they drew their weapons, bringing them to full size as they waited for their adversaries to come into the light. They were confident and ready.

Out came a rat, a dog and a raven. The next thing Advik knew was an intense spike of pain in his right leg. The dog had bitten through his jeans and latched itself onto his calf. He screamed and tried to shake it off before Samar's sword came down, missing it by an inch as the dog disappeared.

In place of the three animals now stood three strange creatures around their height. Thin and lanky, with bold tattoos on their necks and upper bodies, they held curved blades in each hand, wore gold chains with large charms around their necks and metal rings around their calves. Despite looking human, there was something about them that was fierce and animal-like — their blood-red eyes, their shape and gait.

As the vicious pashurivas attacked with their curved blades, the children managed to dodge their weapons and roll over, just as Narada had taught them in their combat training.

Advik quickly picked himself up and shot an arrow at the demon who was about to strike Riya. It grazed the pashuriva on the shoulder, startling him, and giving Riya enough time to get up.

She hurled her spear with precision, and it hit the demon in the chest. He yelled in agony, and as he saw the green discharge from his wound, he was enraged. Samar, meanwhile, was deftly using his sword against the pashuriva that was fighting him.

One of the pashurivas lunged at Advik to take another swing at him. Advik ducked and missed the hit. He quickly let fly an arrow that hit the pashuriva on his legs causing him to fall. "We can't let these puny monsters win!" Fired up by Advik's words, Riya pulled her spear out of the wounded demon and pierced him again. The two pashurivas were on on the ground, critically injured and oozing green slime.

Samar was having a hard time. Advik rushed to help him and shot an arrow. The demon was surprised by the sudden attack but still managed to cut Samar's shoulder with his curved blade. Riya saw her brother in pain and was overcome by rage.

"Samar, fall back! You're bleeding," Riya yelled loudly. "Don't worry. This demon will not escape!" She charged him like a bull and, with one mighty strike, the pashuriva crashed to the forest floor. She continued to punch him, rendering him nearly unconscious. Samar rushed forward, pulling her off the demon. All three pashurivas couldn't fight any more. They just lay on the ground groaning in pain.

Riya rushed over to check on Samar's wound. "Put some pressure on it so that the bleeding stops." Samar just shrugged his shoulders. He felt he could do anything; that nothing in the world could harm him. The wound was insignificant compared to what they had just done.

"We did it," Samar said, raising his hand for a high-five. Advik joined him. Riya hugged Samar and Advik without saying a word.

"What shall we do with them?" Advik asked taking a deep breath.

"First they have to tell us where Naradamuni is." Samar was raring to go. He rested the tip of his sword on the chest of the pashuriva closest to him. "Where is Naradamuni? What did you do with him?" he demanded.

The demon said something but it was so faint, no one could understand him.

"Speak loudly, we can't hear you," Samar shouted, pressing the sword down just a little. The pashuriva felt the pain and closed his eyes. Advik pulled another arrow and pointed it at him. The demon lifted his finger and pointed at the cave.

"It looks like Naradamuni is still inside. Let's go get him," Samar said as he looked at Advik and Riya. They kept their weapons ready and slowly started walking towards the cave.

The captive

The cave was pitch dark and seemed to stretch endlessly. The kids carefully stepped inside and switched on their torches. A bat flew over their heads as the light beams hit the ceiling. It made the cave appear more menacing.

All three of them were scared, but no one wanted to admit that. After walking a few metres they heard a noise, like the rattling of chains followed by the sound of someone groaning.

The children rushed ahead, hoping they would find Narada. The light of their torches fell on him, bruised and chained to the walls of the cave. "Narayan, Narayan!" The familiar but weak chanting fell on the ears of the three children.

"You're here!" Riya shouted. "How did this happen? Why didn't you disappear from here before they could do all of this? How did they get you imprisoned like this? Why didn't the gods help?" Questions poured out from Riya.

"I know you have a lot of questions," Narada replied with a feeble smile. "It all happened so fast that I didn't get any time to react. The raven lifted me so suddenly and threw me down here at the cave. The dog that chased me was barking ferociously, and I was frozen in fear. The rat bound me in these chains. The three are pashurivas, demons who can shapeshift."

"Don't worry, we defeated the creatures, just like you taught us. We left them lying in the dust — licking their wounds," Samar said proudly as he and Advik pulled the chains apart and freed Narada, who couldn't even stand up on his own. "But Naradamuni, what puzzles me is that you could have vanished using your powers, but here you are, a captive of the demons." Riya was still not convinced.

"For some reason, I couldn't use my powers against them. I don't know why," Narada replied. "I faintly remember the raven pashuriva sprinkling something on me, and I couldn't recall any of my powers. They hurt me in the hope that I would talk, but I don't think I said anything."

"Hopefully, you will remember everything once we go back," Advik said as he and Samar helped Narada walk out of the cave. The cave didn't look as frightening on the way out .The sunlight felt reassuring.

"Where are the pashurivas? They were lying here wounded and leaking green ooze. And now, there are just three holes in the ground where they were lying. Did they go underground?" Advik asked.

"Leaving them by themselves was a bad idea. One of us should have stayed back," Riya added. "But what could we have done anyway?"

"I don't know, but where do you think they are now?" wondered Advik.

"Well, they were injured pretty badly. I think they are just hiding. We need to get out of here now," Samar urged. "Maybe they've gone back to Rasatala to report to Harkasura."

"In that case, we need to solve the puzzles faster. Once Harkasura finds out about us, we won't have a lot of time." Advik understood the urgency of the situation. "But first let's get Naradamuni to safety."

"Let's go to the temple and tell Panditji what happened. He might be worried about not finding us in his house. And he can help Naradamuni. You guys take him to the small room in the temple where we met Panditji before, and I will ask him to meet us there," Riya suggested.

Advik and Samar nodded. Advik closed his eyes and chanted the Vayu mantra once again. A strong gust of wind picked them all up and dropped them near the temple. This time round the children were more comfortable flying in the air.

Advik and Samar helped Narada walk to the small room, while Riya rushed to get Pandit Ramashankar. Advik pushed open the door and slowly seated Narada down on one of the chairs. He was already looking better, and it seemed that what the raven had sprinkled on him was beginning to lose effect as well.

"Narayan, Narayan!" he uttered. Hearing his usual chant and cheery tone, Advik felt immensely relieved that Narada was getting back to normal.

Ramashankar burst into the room with Riya, and his eyes grew wide. The celestial sage Narada in jeans and a

T-shirt, battered and bruised? Narada saw the disbelief in his eyes, and before the aged priest could say anything, he bowed his head and returned to his usual form — veena and all. His eyes and smile were bright, if tired. Ramashankar folded his hands and knelt before him.

"Muni, is that you? I don't know what to believe anymore. I never imagined that I would ever meet you in person."

"Narayan, Narayan!" Narada blessed him.

Mystery of the giant

Pandit Ramashankar touched Narada's feet, and tears of joy rolled down his cheek. Narada helped him get up and then, in a flash, went back to his jeans and T-shirt look. Turning to Advik, he said, "Tell me, Advik, what happened while I was away?"

Advik quickly recounted their adventures — how they came to the temple, how Ramashankar helped them by giving them a place to stay, how they found the tablet, the first riddle, the first arrow, and the second riddle in the tablet. "And we don't understand what it means. It seems like gibberish," he finished.

"What does it say?" Narada asked.

Advik took out the metal piece from his backpack. Narada read the inscription loudly.

भूरिभिर्भारिभिर्भीराभू भारैरभिरेभिरे ।

भेरिरेभिभिरभ्राभैरभीरुभिरिभैरिभाः ॥

bhuribhirbhaaribhirbhiraabhu bhaarairabhirebhire.
bheriebhibhirabhraabhairabhirubhiribhairibhaah.

"What do you think this means, Muni?" Advik asked. "We couldn't figure it out. But to be fair, we haven't spent a lot of time on this, either."

"Muni, isn't this an example of vamacitra?" Ramashankar said suddenly. Seeing the blank faces of the children, he explained. "Vamacitras are verses written with a certain use of consonants. I think this is an example that uses only two consonants (bha) and (ra)."

"You are right. I think this is indeed a good riddle in the vamacitra form." Narada closed his eyes for a moment and then opened them again. "I think it translates to something like, 'the fearless elephant, who was like a burden to the earth with its monstrous weight, whose sound was like a kettle-drum, and who was like a dark cloud, attacked the enemy elephant'."

"What? I don't understand the riddle at all!" Advik was bewildered. "What elephant is this referring to?"

"I think this refers to Supratika." Narada seemed to have all the answers.

"Muni, you are right. The reference to Supratika makes sense. He was after all, the most feared elephant," Ramashankar agreed.

"Who is Supratika? Do you know, Samar and Riya?" Advik looked at the two of them. They shook their heads.

"Supratika was the mighty elephant of Bhagadatta, the ruler of the eastern kingdom of Pragjyotisha at the time of the Mahabharata, in what is now Assam. Bhagadatta fought in the war, on the side of the Kauravas. He was extremely skilled in using elephants in warfare. He had a giant, powerful and an almost undefeatable elephant, Supratika," Narada explained.

"I haven't heard this story before. I don't think it was in the Mahabharata series I saw on television with my parents." Advik had exhausted all his resources.

"Well, looks like this is the time to learn more." Narada smiled. "It all happened on the twelfth day of the Mahabharata war. Duryodhana, the Kaurava prince, sent a big elephant division to attack Bhima, the strongest of the Pandavas. But Bhima killed all the elephants with his mace. Enraged by this, Bhagadatta — riding on Supratika — thundered towards Bhima. Supratika killed another elephant that tried to intervene, then crushed Bhima's chariot to pieces, and the horses carrying the chariot ran off in different directions. Faced with the powerful elephant, Bhima swung his mace and injured it. The angry animal then swept him off the ground with his trunk and tried to crush him under its feet.

"What happened next? How did Bhima escape?" Samar was very curious.

"Bhima escaped Supratika's hold and hid behind the ruins of his chariot. Other warriors from the Pandavas' side attempted to come to his rescue and stop Supratika, but they weren't able to help. Finally, Arjuna came to fight Bhagadatta. He started by killing the guards protecting the elephant's legs. Next, an epic battle between two great warriors ensued. Arjuna's arrows were able to break the spear attack by Bhagadatta. Arjuna also broke Supratika's armour with three arrows and then, with a longer arrow, killed the elephant. That was the end of Supratika."

"That is a fascinating story. But how does that help us?" Advik asked, full of doubt.

"Advik, you always have a question mark on your forehead." Samar never gave up a chance to pull his leg.

"But it is an honest question. I'm not just —" Advik began, getting riled up.

"I may know how that makes sense," Ramashankar interrupted. "There is folklore that says Arjuna removed the tusks from the giant elephant and later buried them near the west entrance gate of the Pandava palace here in Hastinapur."

Ascent to Bhuloka

The news about the return of the pashurivas spread through Rasatala like a wildfire. Asuras started to crowd near the ironstone fort to find out what they had learned.

On Harkasura's orders, Sambara brought the demons to the central court hall, and Virata and Tiraka followed. The usual quiet of the hall gave way to slow, rumbling whispers around the room.

When Sambara entered the room with the pashurivas, who were not in their animal form, Virata and Tiraka took their places to the right of the throne, and a hush fell over the room. The crowd strained to get a good glimpse of the three who would stand before Harkasura. Their wounds were still fresh, and they limped as Sambara pushed them through the crowd and to the front of the hall. Virata and Tiraka shot questioning glances at Sambara, who shook his head, signalling them to keep quiet.

The murmuring persisted until the sound of a trident scraping against the floor silenced everyone. The sound drew closer as Harkasura entered the room, looking piercingly around at everyone. All eyes in the room immediately plummeted to the floor. No one dared meet his gaze as he made his way slowly to the throne.

Slamming his trident on the floor as he stepped up to the throne, he turned to face Sambara.

"On your recommendation, I sent these creatures to Bhuloka. Look at them now. What did they expect coming back to Rasatala? That I would be happy? That I would reward them after getting beaten by humans?" Harkasura growled in a furious voice. The flames and smoke billowing from his mouth made him look even more terrifying.

"My lord, it is indeed disgraceful that they lost to humans, but they've come back with vital information. The humans are getting close to invoking the Pashupatastra."

Harkasura, whose patience was thin, blew a small ball of fire in the direction of the pashurivas. They flinched, but before it could reach them, it dissipated. Frustration was plain on his face, but he decided to hear what the demons had to say. "Okay, let's hear what they've learned."

The pashurivas looked at one another briefly before the other two nudged the raven-demon to the front. He nervously recounted that he had heard the mention of Harkasura by a child and followed them to Hastinapur. He had abducted the adult travelling with the children with the hope of finding more information. But the children had tracked him, and used a mantra to follow him back to their base of operations. He told of how they had lost in combat to the three children.

Harkasura, who had been listening with seething rage, now exploded.

"You lost to human children!" he said in a deafening roar. "You have brought shame to all of us with your lack of judgment and your severe lack of fighting skills. Why did you not bring the adult to me when you captured him?"

"My lord, we wanted more information, and we thought that we could get that out of the adult ourselves," the rat-demon spoke in a meek voice.

"You thought? Who told you to think? Did you forget what I said before you left?"

"Lord, please forgive us. This mistake won't happen next time," the dog-demon pleaded with Harkasura.

"Next time! Do you think that after all this, there will be a next time? You are a disgrace," Harkasura thundered and threw his trident.

It went spinning towards the dog pashuriva, severed his head, and returned to Harkasura's hand. Watching the green ooze erupt and splatter in the centre of the court, the remaining pashurivas looked on in terror. The rest of the asuras too watched in horror the sight of Harkasura slaying one of their own. Of course, they dared not say anything against him.

"Please spare me, my Lord. I will do anything you want," the rat-demon begged. "I will be your servant until the end of time."

"I don't need someone who fails in their battles," Harkasura said as he threw the trident again and killed him. The raven-demon turned into a raven and tried to escape, but Harkasura grabbed him in a flash before he had a chance to fly away.

"This is what happens when you defy my orders and bring humiliation to the mighty asuras. How are we going to take over the universe like this? Failure will not be tolerated," Harkasura growled as he crushed the raven in his palms. The last cawing of the raven was deeply disturbing, but no one uttered a single word.

"It appears that these human children are strong and the gods have trusted them with invoking the Pashupatastra, and when they do, that will be the end of us. We need to stop them before they get to their goal and, in order to do that, we must get to Bhuloka. The time we've all been waiting for has arrived. Rasatala will no longer be our home — our prison. Everyone will quake with fear as we take Bhuloka that is rightfully ours. The time has come for the asuras to rule the world!" Harkasura triumphantly slammed his trident on the stone floor.

"Hail Lord Harkasura! Hail Lord Harkasura!" the demons chanted waving their weapons in the air.

"We march tomorrow. We will show the universe that no one can defeat the asuras. Prepare for the final victory." Harkasura raised his trident and blew a big ball of fire from his mouth. Hundreds of asuras yelling and flashing their weapons was definitely a sight to fear.

West gate

Once they were fed and rested, the children and Narada set out with Ramashankar to find the west gate of the ancient Pandava palace. Advik carried the tablet, the arrow, the metal piece and the book of mantras, as well as his bow and arrows.

Narada had returned to his usual, serene self. His bruises had healed. He recalled seeing the Pandava palace some centuries ago. The exact location of the west gate, however, eluded him.

As they walked through the jungle, it was almost sunset. They needed to get to the ruins while there was still light, as the overgrown wilderness would make navigating difficult in the dark. They squeezed through the wire fence around the Department of Forests area, and continued on their route to the palace ruins.

"Aren't you supposed to have the greatest memory of all time? You have seen everything for centuries, and you don't forget things," Advik said to Narada as they walked westwards.

"Yes my boy, but it's hard to find the exact location, now that the great floods of the river Ganga destroyed the palace. There is hardly anything left of it now."

"Then how can we be sure that what Arjuna buried near the west gate is still there?" Advik's questions didn't stop.

"Again, do we have any other alternative, Advik?" Riya snapped back. "We have to believe that Vrishaketu somehow ensured that it would be there, long after natural disasters in his time and beyond."

Advik just shook his head and puckered his lips. He knew that he had to believe in what Riya just said.

"What do you remember about the palace from your last visit?" Ramashankar asked Narada. "Maybe that will help."

"Narayan, Narayan! Where to begin! There was a black stone wall around the palace that stood no less than the height of twenty elephants stacked on top of each other. In each of the four corners stood a watch tower, and archers stood along the wall to protect it. There were two gates; one on the east side and one on the west," Narada said, his eyes appearing lost.

"The west gate was beautiful," he continued. "It had doors that were ten yards wide and equally as tall. They had great, iron spikes on them to stop war elephants from charging in. They could only be opened by a team of men using ropes and pulleys. Great sculptures of Krishna and Shiva decorated the wall, and also carved into it were two elephant heads with blazing eyes that were said to scare off enemies." Narada fell silent.

The kids were listening carefully. "What else do you remember, anything specific to the west gate?" Advik asked again.

"Oh yes, one more thing. The road to the gate was paved with white stones. At the beginning of the road, away from the gate, was a white stone shed that supplied water to travellers approaching the palace. The stones of the road were so bright that you could find your way in the dark just by following the path. The stones bore the marks of the chariots and horses that passed through the gate. On either side of the road beautiful trees welcomed a newcomer."

"I can almost see the gate in front of my eyes," Samar said.

"Maybe the stone-paved road survived. Let's look for it," Advik suggested. "Most likely we won't find the entire road, but any stones with chariot marks on the west side will help us." He was sure he was onto something.

"Good starting point, Advik," Narada agreed. "Let's look for the road."

Along the way, Riya suddenly stopped walking. Pointing enthusiastically to some ruins, she exclaimed, "Don't you think those are the remains of a water shed?"

"You are right Riya; those do look like the foundation stones of the shed." Narada was excited too.

"The paved road should be close. Look at our shadows; they are the longest at this point." Everyone looked at her and then looked around. It was hard to assess where they were, other than the fact that the setting sun was right behind them. Green trees surrounded the area, making it hard to spot any signs of ruins from the ancient times

They frantically looked around before the sun disappeared, but found nothing. Narada had been trying to remember other clues that would have helped in locating the west gate, but he didn't succeed.

In a short while, the whole area slowly began to descend into darkness.

Last piece of the puzzle

"We'd better head back home while we can still see," Ramashankar suggested. "It will be easy to get lost in the dark because of these trees. Our torches will be useless too." The children were disappointed to turn back.

"Naradamuni, can't you create more light for us?" Riya asked.

Before Narada could say anything, he heard Advik yell. "What is that?" The others looked to where his finger pointed to something on the ground a little further away. Advik rushed towards it, and sure enough, a white stone stuck in the ground was shining in the dark. Looking closely he could see marks on it. The others gathered around.

"It does look like the stone from the road to the west gate," Narada confirmed.

"Look I found another one," Samar screamed. "And one more." Samar was ecstatic.

"This has to be the road you were talking about, Naradamuni!" Eyes shining, Riya went quickly down some way to see how many more such stones she could find. There were ten or so of them that for some reason were not visible in daylight, but gleamed white as darkness fell.

"I don't see any more of them," Riya shouted out.

"The west gate must be close to here then."

"Narayan, Narayan!" Narada said happily. "But I don't know where Arjuna buried the tusks of Supratika."

"You described the carvings of the two elephant heads on the gate. What if the tusks were buried under the carvings?" Advik offered.

"Hmm... I like what you propose Advik," Narada affirmed while trying to remember the gate of the palace. He walked a few times from left to right, in deep thought and then pointed to a spot on the left, where the elephant carving was likely to be buried. A few paces away, to the right, he stopped and said with conviction, "I am quite sure that the other carving was here."

"That sounds good but how are we going to dig in this dark?" Samar asked.

"Leave that to me," Narada closed his eyes and uttered something. A big ball of light appeared along with a few massive shovels. "These should make your job easy."

The children wondered if they would even be able to lift the shovels, but were ready to do whatever work was needed to get them to their next answer. Each of them picked up a shovel and to their surprise, they turned out to be feather-light.

"Wow! These are not as heavy as they look," Samar said.

Ramashankar too picked up a shovel. Old as he was, he wanted to help. With one blow, he created a big hole in the ground where Narada had suggested they would find the carving on the left. "I didn't know I was Baahubali!" he said, surprised. Samar and Riya laughed loudly, while Advik stared blankly. The joke about the Indian film was lost on him.

"You need to watch some Hindi movies, Advik," Samar ribbed him as usual.

"I will do that when I feel like it. But now I think your funny brain needs to focus on the job at hand," Advik made a poor comeback.

"Oh no, someone's feelings got hurt," Samar continued.

"Guys, cut it out. Let's try to find the tusks," Riya said, exasperated. Advik and Riya rushed to the right, while Samar joined Ramashankar on the left and began digging hard. Narada watched from a distance.

"Hey!" Samar suddenly yelled. "My spade is hitting against something — something hard." The others rushed over. Advik lay flat on the ground to lean forward and touch it. His hand just about reached it. "It feels solid," he said, knocking on it. "Not like a rock, though."

"This may be it. Advik give me a hand; we need to dig around it carefully to loosen the dirt." As Samar and Adivk knocked off the dirt around it, something long and whitish emerged. It was a giant tusk almost as tall as them! They pulled it out carefully, with help from Narada.

Running her hands up and down the tusk, Riya exclaimed, "Look, there is something in the tusk. I think we found the second arrow." She pulled out a bronze shaft from the hollow in the tusk. "Oh! This is only half of the arrow. Maybe the other half is in the other tusk? So now we need to find that as well!" she said, feeling deflated. Advik and Samar rushed to where Advik had been working and started to dig vigorously again. At first, they didn't find anything. So they called the others. "Let's expand the area and dig a bigger hole." Advik was pumped up.

After a few tries, Advik hit something in the ground. "Yay! I think we've found the second one!" he cheered. They knew what to do this time. With Ramashankar's help, they pulled it out of the ground, praying that the other half of the arrow would be in it. After some anxious searching, Riya eased out the rest of the arrow. She aligned the two parts of the dart and pressed them together. An electric spark zipped through the arrow and Riya dropped it in fright.

"Now that is what I am talking about. We are two-thirds of the way there everyone!" Advik raised his fist in the air and picked up the arrow. He hurriedly opened his backpack and took out the tablet. He inserted the arrow in the second hole and turned it clockwise.

With the sound of gears turning, another metal piece dropped onto the ground. Riya, now familiar with the pattern, picked it up and stared at it. Advik removed the arrow from the hole and secured it in his backpack.

"Just one moment," Ramashankar interrupted gently. "Now that we have found it, should we take it home and make sense of it? We've been away a long time, and everyone at home will be getting worried." The kids were tired too, so they reluctantly agreed.

"Narayan, Narayan! I will let you guys get some rest. Call me when you are ready for treasure hunting again." Narada smiled.

"But before you go, can you have the flash of light guide us all the way back home?" Advik requested.

"Narayan, Narayan! As you wish." He smiled and disappeared. The others started walking back home with the flash of light leading the way.

Can't stand my ground

Everyone was exhausted after a day full of adventures, fights and solving clues. They decided to look at the new clue in the morning with a fresh set of eyes. That night, it took Advik a long while to fall asleep. He missed his parents terribly and wondered how Maya Advik was doing in his place. Had they any idea at all that he wasn't there? How would they react if they knew that he was on an adventure — a scary one, against fierce asuras — to save the world. What would happen if he didn't return safely? Would the Maya Advik continue to be there? But he didn't want to think about that. He had to save the world and his grandfather.

He drifted into a restless sleep, till he felt he was being shaken awake. He tried to pull the blanket closer and go back to sleep, but the shaking wouldn't stop.

"I don't want to get up just yet. Leave me alone," he shouted, but the shaking got worse. Awake now, he could hear dogs barking and birds shrieking. The crows in the neighborhood seemed to have gone wild, cawing loudly. It felt like the earth was rumbling under him.

"Earthquake!" Advik jumped up and remembered to grab his backpack before he dashed out of the room. Riya,

Samar and Ramashankar's family were all running out of the house as well. A few seconds later, the rumbling and trembling stopped, and it went all quiet.

"What just happened? Was that an earthquake? How big was it? I am worried about my family," Advik questioned. "It was terrifying."

Let me check if there is a report on the television," Ramashankar said as he went back inside to turn it on in the living room. The kids followed him there. There was a news flash acknowledging the tremors, but no further information was available. The seismologists didn't have any data about the sudden quake.

"That is strange. I guess it will take some more time before they can find the cause of the tremors," Ramashankar said, turning down the volume.

"Maybe Naradamuni knows," Samar suggested. "He knows everything that is happening. I am sure he can tell us more."

"That is a good idea. Let me call Muni," Advik agreed with Samar for a change. The three of them went with Ramashankar to his room and closed the door. Advik closed his eyes, folded his hands and chanted "Narayan, Narayan!" A giant spark of light appeared in front of them, and Narada appeared.

"I was about to pay you a visit, anyway," Narada said with a worried face. "You experienced the earth shaking under your feet?"

Everyone nodded and waited anxiously for him to reveal the cause. "I woke up because of that earthquake," Advik said.

"It was no earthquake. The tremors were caused by Harkasura's demon army trying to break through to

Bhuloka from Rasatala…" Narada paused so that everyone could digest what he had just said.

"What? That's terrible news. How long will it be before they break through?" Advik asked anxiously.

"Well, I can't say for sure, but I don't think we have much time to find a way to invoke the Pashupatastra. If we fail, the earth and the human race are in grave danger," Narada replied.

"Muni, I think that is too much pressure for these children. Can't the gods do something to help?" Ramashankar looked around at his new, small, terrified friends.

"If the gods get involved, then we risk losing Bhuloka and Swargaloka to Harkasura. The gods can create more obstacles in the way of the demon army, but I am not sure how much more time that will buy us. We need to do it ourselves," Narada replied with a grim face.

"In that case, we need to solve this quickly. What do you think of this second riddle?" Advik asked as he handed the metal piece to Narada.

निध्वनज्जवहारीभा भेजे राग रसात्तम: ।
ततमानवजारासा सेना मानिजनाहवा ।।

Nidhvanajjavahaaribhaa bheje raaga rasaattamha.
Tatamaanavajaaraasaa senaa maanijanaahavaa.

Narada read the inscription out loudly.

"What does it mean, Muni?" Riya asked.

"It means something like this: 'That great army, with majestic and trumpeting elephants of high speed, and people filling the battlefield with their triumphant roar, suddenly became ferocious with anger in that battle of proud heroes'."

"That doesn't make any sense. No clues have been straightforward. Why would the last one be any different," Advik groaned.

"Maybe Vrishaketu got tired of building the complex clues and finally decided to make our life easy. Maybe we are overthinking it," said Samar.

"No, Samar. It can't be so simple. Plus, what's easy about it? What makes the great army ferocious? I don't remember any incident in the Mahabharata that mirrors this description. What do you think, Muni?" Riya punted the question back to Narada.

Narada closed his eyes and opened them after a few moments. "I looked at all the days of the war again, but I can't find anything that matches the description."

"Muni, what about the fall of Abhimanyu, do you think that fits the description?" Ramashankar suggested. When Arjuna's son was killed brutally by the Kauravas, the Pandavas must have been full of anger."

"No. After the incident, the Pandava warriors began to shed tears. Yudhishthira, the eldest Pandava fainted, and with great effort was brought back to consciousness. All the famed warriors then gathered around Yudhishthira and mourned the injustice in the war."

"Maybe there is some clue hidden in this inscription that we are missing," Advik continued to insist. "But I'm not sure what."

"Oh wait, do you think it will make sense if we take every second or third word of the inscription?" Samar had a sudden idea.

Riya looked at him with surprise. "I was about to suggest that too."

Narada quickly thought about what Samar said and shook his head. "No, that doesn't mean anything to me." He shrugged his shoulders. Ramashankar was lost in thought still trying combinations.

"What do we do now?" Advik felt his confidence drain away. Riya put an arm around him as she noticed the look on his face. Samar too held Riya's hand. The team was running out of time.

# Vidura ka tila

Half an hour went by, and they had come no closer to solving the riddle. Advik sulked down to the floor and mindlessly made circles with his index finger. They felt light tremors again under their feet.

The three children looked at each other. The end was near, and they couldn't stop it.

"Why did Vrishaketu have to make it so complex?" Samar went from being dejected to being agitated. Advik and Riya had the same feeling but didn't say anything. Narada and Ramashankar strained their memories about other wars to which the inscription could be referring, but came up with nothing.

Advik continued to move his finger in circles, first clockwise, then counter-clockwise.

"Wait!" Riya screamed at the top of her lungs. Everyone was startled. "What if the inscription has to be read the other way round?"

Everyone looked confused.

"I mean, look how Advik is moving his finger in circles. What happens if we read the inscriptions backwards, does that mean anything?" Riya posed a question to Narada and Ramashankar.

"Are you thinking the inscription is a palindrome?" Advik asked.

"If it is a palindrome, then it will mean the same thing, but if we read this one in reverse, will we get another shloka?"

"Let's try," said Narada.

वाहनाजनि मानासे साराजावनमा ततः।
मत्त सारगराजेभे भारिहावज्जन ध्वनि।।

Vaahanaajani maanase saaraajaavanamaa tataha.
Matta saaragaraajebhe bhaarihaavajjana dhvani.

"It indeed makes sense, Riya. It means, 'And after this, that great army, which is capable of destroying the pride of the enemies and which has never experienced defeat, marched towards the enemy with strong and maddened elephants and people roaring in enthusiasm and jubilation.' What do you think?" Narada questioned Ramashankar.

"It seems to me to be the start of the battle," mused Ramashankar. "Since it's an army that has never experienced defeat. But what is so important about the beginning of the war?"

"Oh I know, I know!" Advik shouted with excitement. "Doesn't it refer to the conch shell they blew before starting the war?" He paused as everyone stared at him with surprise. "Don't give me that look. I know my Mahabharata too. Isn't it referring to the conch shell that Lord Krishna had?"

"Narayan, Narayan! That is very good, Advik, and you do know your Mahabharata." Narada smiled. "You think it refers to the Panchajanya, Krishna's conch shell that he blew to start the Mahabharata war?"

"Yes, Muni. But where does that lead us?" Advik was stumped again.

"Hmm... Let's see... After the war was over, Krishna gave the conch shell to Vidura, who was the adviser to the kings of Hastinapur. He hid the conch in an underground pillar supporting the palace so that the painful memories of the war would fade away."

"Vidura's palace used to be on what is now Vidura ka tila on a small hill on the banks of the Burhganga River near here," Ramashankar said. "The government did some excavations at the site and found something buried in the ground, but they stopped work for unknown reasons and declared the area protected."

"That must be it; I think it must be the pillar that we are looking for." Advik was elated once again.

"If the archaeological team couldn't dig it out, how are we going to do it?" Advik wondered.

"Well, we do have more help than them." Advik smiled and looked at Narada.

"Narayan, Narayan!" Narada smiled back. "Let's go find the last arrow and unlock the mantra for the Pashupatastra before the demons make their way to Bhuloka. Panditji, can you take us to Vidura ka tila?"

"Sure, make sure you have everything that you need," Ramashankar said. The twins packed their weapons into their backpacks. Advik stuffed his with the arrows, the metal pieces, the stone tablet, and his own bow and arrows. They stepped out of the house for the final quest as the ground trembled and shook.

Strategy for war

Sambara rushed to meet Harkasura along with Virata and Tiraka. Harkasura was reclining on the ironstone throne with his trident, devising strategy for the war. He was staring at a rock in his right hand that had the map of the earth on it. The demon army was close to breaking out of Rasatala and getting onto the earth's surface. Mass hysteria had overtaken the minds of the demons as they believed that Harkasura was the saviour who was going to lead them to eternal glory.

Sambara, Virata and Tiraka kneeled down before Harkasura. He was annoyed by the interruption, and unwillingly looked at the stooped trio.

"My lord, I have a suggestion for you," Sambara said softly.

"Hmm! What is it that you want to say?"

"My lord, I don't think you should stand in the front of the army just yet."

"Why? Why do you say that? You don't think I can lead the army?" Harkasura picked up his trident and growled.

"No, my lord, that is not what I meant. You are our saviour; we need you to conquer the world. I am afraid, however; it is critical that we have the Pashupatastra in our hands before we attack the human race."

"You think those puny children can invoke the mighty Pashupatastra? They won't even know how to use it or control its power. The gods are fools. They trust these tiny humans to stop the mighty Harkasura. I only pity their brains."

"You are right, my lord. But," Sambara tried to convince Harkasura, "at least let Virata and Tiraka lead from the front, so they can crush the human children and get the Pashupatastra for you. After that, nothing stops us from accomplishing your vision of total annihilation of the gods from the universe," Sambara pleaded his case. Virata and Tiraka too nodded in agreement.

Harkasura thought for a while and came to terms with what Sambara was suggesting. The more he thought about it, the more he began to like the idea. After all, even if the children were successful in their quest, they would have to use the Pashupatastra on Virata or Tiraka, and they wouldn't be able to use it again on Harkasura. No one could stop him in his conquest after that. A slight smile appeared on his dragon face. He was going to benefit from it, no matter what.

"Okay, I think what you are suggesting makes sense," he said with a low growl. "You two must make sure that you don't do anything stupid and hurt yourselves. Now go to the front lines and get me the Pashupatastra."

"Yes, my lord," Tiraka and Virata said in unison as they prepared to get up. Harkasura banged his trident on the floor. "Sambara, I wish to speak with you alone."

Sambara stayed back as Virata and Tiraka left the court. Harkasura tossed the rock with the map of the earth to

Sambara. He caught it clumsily, and Harkasura laughed at his awkwardness.

"Given that the human children are in Hastinapur, I think we will have to break through to Bhuloka there. Once we get rid of them, we should march west. When humans realise what's happened, they will try to use their weapons to stop us, but nothing will match our might. We will enslave them, and that will force the gods to jump in. I will kill the gods and establish the rightful rule of asuras over Bhuloka and Swargaloka. What do you think of that plan?"

"That is an excellent plan, my Lord. I think we should get the humans to surrender to us by killing a few thousands of them to demonstrate our strength. That will scare the gods and force them to join the battle to save the humans."

"Now you are thinking like an asura who wants to rule the world. If we do it right, victory will soon be ours, and we will rule the world for eternity." Harkasura laughed loudly.

Sambara too laughed with him. Finally, his plan to resurrect Harkasura was going to restore the glory of the asuras, and Sambara would go down in history as the most celebrated strategist ever known. Somewhere at the back of his mind, however, he feared that the puny children were going to be a problem. His new strategy to fight with Virata and Tiraka in front, he felt, would address that threat.

He bowed to Harkasura again. "It is only a matter of time before the world kneels before the great Harkasura."

"You are smart, Sambara. Now, get ready to conquer earth," Harkasura said, pounding his trident.

Tick-Tock... Boom

The three children ran toward Vidura ka tila along the banks of the Burhganga River, where once the palace of the wisest man of his time stood. After the Kurukshetra war, he had retired to a life of quiet prayer in the forest. The hill had a few trees, but beneath it, was a thick tree cover that gave it the feel of a jungle.

"We need to move fast, the clock is ticking," said Advik impatiently. He felt the pressure mounting as the shock waves beneath them grew stronger. It was not going to be long before the demon army made its way above.

From an outsider's view, it would have been a strange sight: three children racing with a priest in bright orange robes, and a tall, distinguished-looking man in jeans and a ponytail following closely behind.

As their feet started to get tired, Samar remembered something. "Advik, you remember the wind mantra? Why don't we use that to get to Vidura ka tila faster?"

"You couldn't have thought of that sooner, you slowpoke?" Advik was both relieved and annoyed.

"At least I remembered it. You two are useless," Samar snapped back. Advik looked at Narada.

Narada shrugged his shoulders and replied, "You know I can't use my powers with you. I can only guide you, but you have to do things yourself. Now, this is good thinking, and we can certainly get there a lot faster with the Vayu mantra."

Advik, Samar, and Riya closed their eyes and began to chant.

A strong gust of wind picked them up and dropped them at their destination. It was a beautiful and quiet place, with the sound of flowing water, a tree-covered hill, and the occasional chirping of a bird flying by. It was easy to imagine living in a palace here.

Advik took a big breath of fresh air. "Come on, let's get going. We need to find the third arrow before the asuras arrive," he said urgently.

In the middle of the mound, they could see a carved rock embedded firmly. Its surface looked like a tabletop, and its four corners were carved into circular lotus petals. They were quite sure that this had to be the underground pillar that once supported the palace.

"We have to hope that the conch is somewhere near the top of the pillar. Vidura wouldn't have gone too deep, would he?" Riya asked doubtfully.

"But how will we find it even if it's near the top?" asked Advik, frustrated at the how much they had to do with so little time. "How do we cut through the stone?"

"Narayan, Narayan!" Narada closed his palms and opened them. A bright cloud appeared for an instant and dropped a long, sharp blade, quite like a sword, on the ground.

Advik picked it up. Unlike the shovel, this was quite heavy, and he almost dropped it. "This can cut through the pillar?" Advik asked Narada.

"Narayan, Narayan! You'll find out," Narada replied.

"Be careful, Advik. You don't want to get hurt, or damage the conch shell either," Riya warned.

Advik nodded and swung the blade. A loud noise disturbed the quiet as the blade sliced through the stone and dislodged the top of it. He put down the blade and lifted the block of stone with great difficulty so that they could look into the pillar. But unable to hold the heavy piece of stone in his hands any longer, Advik dropped it and it fell with a thud. Samar tried to push the block of stone away, but it was too heavy. Riya and Ramashankar joined in. Together, they managed to push it over and a cloud of dust rose from the earth.

Everyone peered into the pillar anxiously, dreading that there could be further obstacles to be sorted out. But no! Inside, was a cleverly carved out shallow space, almost like a basin. And there, sitting snugly, was a giant, pearly-white conch!

"We did it, we got it!" Advik was ecstatic. He raised his palm and Samar gave him a high-five instantly. They were thrilled. Riya reached into the hole and carefully picked up the conch with both hands.

"Is this the Panchajanya?" Ramashankar asked disbelievingly, and Narada nodded. Ramashankar touched it reverently to his forehead.

"I found the last arrow," Advik yelled as he pulled it out from inside the conch while Riya held it. The trio was complete. "Samar, can you get the tablet from my backpack?" Samar quickly brought it out.

They all held their breath as Advik inserted the third arrow into the last remaining hole and turned it clockwise. The levers turned inside, and with a cracking noise, the tablet split in half. Advik opened the two halves with trembling hands. It was the moment that he had dreamt about.

Inside the stone tablet, was an intricate system of levers and gears that allowed the two inscribed metal pieces with the first and second clues to come out of the tablet. Finally, at the bottom, was a string of letters carved in the stone. Advik handed the tablet to Narada.

"Is that the mantra for the Pashupatastra?" he asked.

Narada looked at them for a moment and replied. "Indeed it is. I am going to read it out to you. Make sure you remember it. To invoke the Pashupatastra, you will need the three arrows and this mantra. So listen carefully," Narada said. Advik put the arrow in his backpack and was all ears.

ॐ नमो भगवते महापाशुपताय तुलबलवीर्य पराक्रमाय।
त्रिपञ्च नयनाय नानारूपाय नानाप्रहरणोद्यताय सर्वांग रक्ताय।।

Om namo bhagavate mahaapaashupataaya
tulabalaveerya paraakramaaya.
Tripancha nayanaaya naanaaroopaaya
naanaapraharanodyataaya sarvaanga raktaaya.

Advik, Samar, and Riya repeated the mantra over and over again with closed eyes to memorise it.

And then, just as they opened their eyes, there was a big explosion.

Boom…! The earth cracked open.

Sacrifice

Virata leaped out, ripping apart two trees that stood in his way. He was so huge that the children couldn't see past his waist. He wore no armour, as none could be forged large enough for him. He wielded a gurz, a round-headed mace with spikes.

Tiraka followed Virata out of Rasatala. He wore full body armour and a metal crown on his bull head that gleamed in the sunlight. Steam billowed from his nostrils as he glared at the children with bright red eyes that matched his outfit. With his enormous muscles and clenched fists, he looked formidable.

Advik, Riya and Samar were terrified. It was one thing to feel brave about saving the world, but quite another to see these behemoths advancing towards them. They began to sweat with fear. Advik trembled so much that the tablet fell from his hands. Samar looked around desperately for a hideout. Riya began to edge backwards.

Ramashankar too stared in horror, the colour draining from his face. But from somewhere within, he found a voice. "Draw your weapons — quickly!" he shouted to the children.

The kids fumbled frantically for them. Ramashankar, who had no weapons at all, stood tall in the thick of things. The children look at Narada. He uttered something and created a dense fog.

"Unfortunately, I can't help you more. This fog will disappear soon. Remember your training and call me if you need anything," Narada said.

Advik lifted his bow. It immediately adjusted to his grip, and he felt a surge of reassurance from within. He looked up and screamed, "Guys, this is it! We've got to fight. Come on, let's get them!"

"Yes! Let's send these guys back to where they belong," Riya shouted back, fully charged as she wielded her spear. "What do you say, Samar?" She flashed him a look to see how he was doing.

"Ha, I am ready too," Samar joined in. "As you said Advik, let's send them packing."

"Is that Harkasura? The bull-headed demon?" Advik asked Narada, as he aimed his bow and took a stance.

"No, he is Tiraka, and the giant is Virata, two of the most feared asuras," Narada called out. "Harkasura must be biding his time. But these two are his strongest and most feared," Narada added before disappearing with the fog.

The children were now visible to the demons. Seeing the size of their opponents, Virata and Tiraka roared with laughter that sounded like thunder from the sky. Uprooting a neem tree with one hand, Virata threw it at the children and Ramashankar. They ducked swiftly and it missed them. But that scared Ramashankar, and he took refuge behind a tree.

Virata charged toward Advik and Samar, swinging his gurz.

Tiraka rushed at Riya with incredible speed, wanting to pierce her with his horns. Riya jumped behind a rock and Tiraka slammed into it. The rock shattered with the impact and Riya was thrown in the air. She hurled her spear that struck Tiraka in his right arm. He laughed uproariously at the wound inflicted by the spear. Pulling it out with his left hand, he flung it back at Riya. She quickly dodged it and escaped.

Virata reached the boys and swung his gurz hard at them. They rolled swiftly to avoid the attack, but the metal spikes grazed their arms. Advik drew two arrows and fired them in rapid succession, hitting Virata's massive legs. He was hoping that he had seriously injured the demon, but Virata only laughed. Samar lunged with his sword, but it seemed to make no difference. Virata bent down and delivered a blow to Samar that sent him flying through the air and crashing to the ground. Although a patch of grass cushioned the fall, the impact made him lose consciousness.

Tiraka, meanwhile, was charging at Riya again, horns lowered. As he reached her, she grabbed the left horn and swung herself upwards, landing on his shoulders. Before he realised what happened, she jumped down and rushed to see her brother.

Advik was now on his own. He shot two sharp arrows at the asuras. One hit Virata in his chest, and he screamed so loudly that Ramashankar had to close his ears. Tiraka, however, grabbed the arrow that headed towards him, broke it in half and threw it away.

"Is that all you've got, you puny human?" Tiraka mocked him. In one great stride, he came up to Advik and grabbed him by the legs, hurling him over to where Samar had been tossed. Trying to land on his feet, Advik felt something in his legs snap.

"I can't stand up! I think I broke my legs," he shrieked. Through the blinding pain, he extracted another arrow and fired it into Tiraka. It struck him right between his eyes. It looked like he had grown a third horn. The impact made him scream loudly but not enough to take him down.

Riya looked helplessly at Advik and Samar. "Samar, get up! We are losing the battle!" She shook Samar vigorously. As he slowly opened his eyes, Virata uprooted another tree and swept the three of them into the Burhganga River.

The demons laughed loudly from the river bank. Still hidden, Ramashankar knew it was time for him to do something. Thinking on his feet, he rushed toward the tablet that was still lying on the ground.

"Here, I have what you want! I've got the tablet that has the mantra to invoke the Pashupatastra. Come and get it!" he provoked the asuras, hoping to distract them and give the children time to escape.

Virata turned and swung his gurz wildly at the priest, who leaped to evade the attack but was not fast enough. The gurz caught him right in the chest and flung him to the ground. He lay breathless and began to bleed profusely, still clutching the tablet.

"Is that all you can do?" he shouted out scornfully. He sensed his time had come and was trying to do what he could to keep the asuras occupied. Tiraka rushed towards him, picked him up with his horns and slammed him on a nearby boulder. That was enough to silence Ramashankar. His lifeless body tumbled to the forest floor, the tablet falling out of his hands. Picking it up, Tiraka noticed the inscription.

"It looks like this old priest has given us the invocation mantra for the Pashupatastra," he said to Virata. "Now no one can stop Harkasura. We asuras will rule the universe."

"What about the children?" Virata questioned. "Should we go look for them?"

"I am sure they've drowned by now. I can't see anything in the river," Tiraka said. "Can you?"

"No," Virata replied. "After what we did to them, there is no chance they can still be alive. Look at what happened to this human," he pointed at Ramashankar and laughed loudly.

Tiraka nodded his head. "Let's go and present this to Harkasura."

"Shall we take the dead body too?"

"What for? Let him lie here and rot," Tiraka sneered, walking back to the unholy opening in the earth's surface.

It's not over till...

Advik thought he was going to die. He had tried to keep himself afloat, but with legs that were useless and a water-filled backpack weighing him down, it was a losing struggle. He was giving up, exhausted, when suddenly a protruding branch caught his backpack. He held onto the branch with whatever will power he could muster. Then he remembered. "Narayan, Narayan!" he called out desperately.

Sure enough, Narada appeared, floating above the water.

"Help us, Muni," Advik mumbled and lost consciousness.

The next thing he hazily knew was that someone was near him, rubbing something on his body and helping him gulp some liquid.

Then he dreamt that Samar, Riya and he had died, and Harkasura had defeated the gods and taken over the world. All of humankind had been enslaved. Advik saw his mother and father being made to heft heavy burdens up a hill under the watchful eye of a terrible demon, who cracked a whip on his father's back, causing him to tumble to the ground. His mother stooped to help him, only to have the next lash on her. And somehow he knew that it was all his fault.

"It's okay, Advik," someone said. "You'll soon be fine." With a sudden jolt, Advik opened his eyes to find himself lying on the ground, looking up at a dark, cloudy, moonless sky. Two men in white robes stood near him. He could see there was light, but couldn't identify from where it came. His backpack was next to him, and he grabbed it.

"Ma, where are you? Where am I? Who are you guys?" he mumbled. A sudden wave of realisation washed over him, and he cried, "Am I dead? What about Samar and Riya? Did Harkasura take over the universe?" The questions tumbled out.

The two men in white slowly turned to him. "No, Advik, you are not dead," they spoke calmly. You are still in Hastinapur, just shielded by a cloud cover. After you asked Narada for help, he summoned us. We are the Ashwinis, the twin doctors of the gods. Samar and Riya are here too. Just behind you. How are you feeling now?"

Advik looked at his leg. It no longer felt broken. He didn't have any bruises on his body either. "I'm feeling fine. What did you do? Did you make me drink something and rub something on my body?"

"Yes," smiled the Ashwinis.

"How long has it been since we fought with Virata and Tiraka?"

"Oh! That fight happened a few hours ago."

"It feels like a long time has passed since then. So Harkasura hasn't taken control of the earth."

"We don't think so, but you should check with Naradamuni. He will have the latest details. Our job is healing."

"Thank you! Thank you for making us well again," Advik said as he got up. He closed his eyes and chanted, "Narayan, Narayan!" and Narada appeared.

"I feel much better, Muni, what is going on? Has Harkasura come to earth?"

"Your fear is correct, my son. Harkasura has made his way to earth. Virata, Tiraka, and Sambara have accompanied him along with the rest of the demon army. From what I see, he is about to burn the jungle and the city of Hastinapur. Once the humans pray to the gods, they will have to intervene, and Harkasura will rout them because he is protected by Shiva's boon. I think that is his plan. He needs to be stopped right away."

Advik heard yawning and turned to see Riya and Samar waking up.

"Advik, what happened? Is Harkasura here?" Samar had the same questions as Advik, who answered them rapidly. Riya and Samar checked their bodies for bruises and wounds, and to their amazement found none. They saw Narada smiling at them and knew that Advik was right.

"But how will we stop Harkasura?"Advik turned to Narada. "We couldn't even stop Virata and Tiraka. They almost killed us."

"Plus it's going to be dark soon. Don't asuras become more powerful in the dark?" Samar added.

"We need to try harder, that's all," said Riya.

"Yes. If we can't stop the demons, they will kill the gods and enslave the humans and flog them. I just saw that in my dreams," Advik persisted.

"And you believed your dream? That is an excellent motivational speech and an obvious call to battle," Samar snickered, getting back to his old self again.

"Samar, this is not the time to be too clever. Advik is right. We need to find a way to stop the demons." Riya suddenly remembered something. "Where is Panditji?"

"Pandit Ramashankar died trying to save your lives," Narada replied gravely, narrating the whole incident.

Tears rolled down their cheeks, and their hearts sank. In just two days Ramashankar had become their close friend, guide, and father figure. Not having him around was going to be a painful reality to accept.

Riya wiped her tears with her sleeves and asked the Ashwinis, "Why can't you bring him back?"

"We can heal, but bringing someone back to life is not for us," one of the doctors replied. The twins looked so similar and were soft-spoken, that it was hard to guess who was talking.

"He made a great sacrifice — not just for you, but a bigger cause. He believed in you and had faith that you can stop Harkasura," Narada comforted the children. "Now you can't let his sacrifice go to waste."

"What can we do? We tried our best and failed. Our failure cost him his life," Riya said as she tried to stop her tears.

"The asuras were too much for us. They were huge and strong. Our weapons didn't even hurt them. How can we win? We've also lost the tablet that had the inscription for the Pashupatastra." Advik used his palms to wipe his tears.

"Are you sure you used all that you have? And don't you remember the inscription? If you do, then you don't need the tablet. All you need are the three arrows, and I believe that those are still in your backpack."

Advik checked if the arrows were there, along with the book of mantras. "I do remember the inscription on the tablet, and I've got the arrows right here," he confirmed.

"But we tried hard, and all we managed to do was inflict a couple of wounds on them," Samar insisted.

"If you managed to hurt them, you can fight them. Think about how you were able to do that," Narada continued. "Every war needs a strategy. What was yours?"

"The asuras took us by surprise. So there was no strategy," Advik said, beginning to understand.

"There is your answer. You need to devise a plan to fight the demons and prove that Pandit Ramashankar wasn't wrong when he gave up his life for you."

The tears had started to dry up, and a new spark appeared in Advik's eyes. "I think I know the weakness of Virata. I don't think he can move fast or see very well. That is how I was able to strike him!" Samar declared proudly. "We can use that against him."

"I don't think Tiraka is very smart. He slammed into a big rock when I jumped out of his way. He did manage to blow up the rock on impact, but I think we can use his lack of intelligence to our advantage," Riya added.

"You are right. You need to not only find the weakness of the enemy but also find the right battleground to fight your war. The demon army easily outnumbers you," Narada warned the kids.

"I think this jungle is a good location for us. We can hide behind the trees and attack. Plus, Harkasura and the demons think we're dead so we can use that to our benefit. We should find a way to get close to Virata and strike him multiple times. And if we can get Tiraka to ram his horns into a tree that he can't uproot, he'll be stuck. That will give us a leg up on them," Advik started to strategise.

"He uprooted a neem tree. Maybe we should try a banyan. It will be very hard to uproot that one," Riya weighed in. Samar nodded.

Thinking more about the battle and finalising details about their plans they felt bolder.

"You know what, it would be good to have an axe in addition to the spear." Riya looked at Narada.

"I want a shield with my sword. And I want the sword to have the same strength as the blade Advik used to cut through the stone," Samar demanded.

"I would like an unlimited supply of arrows that can pierce anything, carry fire, and explode when they hit the target." Advik went a little nuts with his wishlist, but if there was ever an appropriate time to make demands of the gods, this was undoubtedly it.

Narada smiled and uttered, "Narayan, Narayan!" The familiar white cloud appeared, and the new weapons clattered to the ground. The children rushed to pick them up and felt a new wave of energy surge through them.

"Now, it's time to take this fight to Harkasura," Advik said, as he extended his right fist to his partners in battle. Riya and Samar bumped their fists against his. Narada smiled and looked at the Ashwinis, who disappeared along with the mystical white light and the clouds surrounding them.

That was when, in the distance, a giant fire began to blaze, threatening to engulf the forest and gobble up Hastinapur.

At war

The wildfire that had been let loose in the forest hissed and howled like a mass of angry snakes gone mad. It was a terrifying sight to behold as the demons raised their weapons and chanted Harkasura's name. Harkasura was examining the stone tablet that Tiraka had brought back.

The children crouched low, sneaking closer to the fire, wondering how they could contain it without alerting Harkasura.

"There must be something we can do to stop the fire, but I don't know what," Samar said looking tense.

"We need a massive amount of water. A monsoon shower would come in handy right about now. Can we make it rain?" Riya asked.

"That gives me an idea. We can summon the rain god Varuna and ask for his help. There must be a mantra in the book," Advik said.

"Won't Harkasura recognise him and try to kill him?" Samar asked.

"You are right, Samar. So we must warn him, but he is our only option to contain the fire right now. What do you guys say?" Advik asked. Riya and Samar both nodded.

Advik opened the book of mantras and handed it over to Riya. She flipped through the pages and found the one for calling Lord Varuna. Eyes closed, she chanted it.

A celestial figure appeared before them riding on a makara, a crocodile.

The three bowed before Varuna, the god of water.

"Lord Varuna, please help. We need to stop the fire that Harkasura and his asuras have started," Advik requested urgently.

"I appreciate the gravity of the situation you are in right now, children. This is a tough battle, to say the least, and I would like to help," Lord Varuna's voice was very calming.

"If Harkasura finds out you are trying to help us defeat him, he will try to attack you too," Samar tried to warn him.

"Thank you, child. I am well aware of Harkasura's feelings toward the gods. I am also very impressed by what you three have accomplished thus far by your bravery and determination, and I daresay it's time the gods chipped in. If I get hurt in the process, so be it. Failing to stop Harkasura would be an even greater loss than my own life. The universe is at risk."

"Once you stop the fire, Harkasura's army will attack whatever they can. But we will be ready. We have a strategy. So please help us, Lord Varuna, and get out of there as quickly as you can," Riya said confidently.

Lord Varuna disappeared and, in the next moment, clouds started to move into the dark sky. The demons were too busy creating mayhem to notice, but the kids knew what was coming and took shelter under a big tree. With a loud thunderclap, it started to rain heavily. The sudden rain caught the asuras by surprise, and they began to scatter.

Some of the demons, in confusion, ran straight into the blaze. Their screams echoed. The kids' plan had sent the demon army into complete disarray.

Harkasura watched enraged as his attack seemed to disintegrate. His army was in a panic, and the fire was dying out under the sudden assault from the sky. He and his three generals set their minds to reigniting the inferno. Under the unabated downpour, however, it was a futile effort.

The rain stopped as soon as the fire was doused. Harkasura realised this was no coincidence. He looked up at the sky and picked up his trident. He paused for a moment and then hurled it into the sky with all his might. It disappeared like a missile and a few seconds later, came down with the makara that Lord Varuna had been riding, but the rain god had managed to escape.

Harkasura grabbed his trident and kicked the wounded makara. He was furious that his plans had had a setback.

"The gods have interfered with our plan. That is a good sign. We won't have to wait long for them all to come down here and then we'll defeat them," Sambara tried to put a positive spin on the chaos.

Harkasura stared at him and, with his left hand, tossed the tablet in the air. With his right hand he threw his trident at the tablet, which exploded into pieces. He growled and blew fire skyward. He then realised something and, with his fiery dragon eyes, slowly looked around.

His eyes scanned everything, even beyond what the other huge asuras could see. They locked onto Advik, who felt a strange tremor go through him. "Guys, I feel funny.

As if someone is looking right into me. It could be Harkasura. Maybe he knows we're here."

The kids stayed close, but it seemed like they could feel Harkasura's eyes following them.

"You said the tiny human kids were dead. But there they are, under the tree. Is this what you meant when you assured me that you took care of them?" Harkasura picked up his trident and growled at Virata and Tiraka.

"My lord, I am not sure how this happened. We saw them drown in the river ourselves." Tiraka was himself surprised. "I will chase them down and bring their dead bodies to you."

"I told you, there is absolutely no room for failures of any kind. You know the consequences."

"My lord, they brought you the invocation mantra for the Pashupatastra, and you have just destroyed it. No one can stop us anymore. What are these kids going to do anyway? Give Virata and Tiraka one more chance to eliminate them once and for all," Sambara tried to plead for his comrades. "These two can do it in their sleep. Once we take care of them, we will attack Hastinapur with all our might."

Virata and Tiraka stood trembling before Harkasura with their heads bowed low, hoping they would escape the fate of the pashurivas.

Harkasura growled, "Go and finish your job. If you fail, I will make an example out of you two."

"Yes my lord," both said in unison and angrily started walking towards the children.

Taking on the warmongers

The kids were locked and loaded for Virata and Tiraka. Riya climbed a banyan tree, Samar scaled up the short neem tree next to it, and Advik waited on the ground in between them. They gripped their weapons tightly. The dark night was looking deadlier, but the kids were determined this time.

"Are you ready, guys?" Advik asked. "Here they come."

"Yes! It's time to annihilate these pests from the face of the earth," Samar said in a rush of adrenaline. Riya smiled grimly. They couldn't see each other's faces clearly, but they were fully coordinated and knew how this needed to go.

Tiraka dug his legs into the ground, lowered his horns and started running towards the children. Virata's thumping steps echoed in the back.

Advik pulled out an arrow that could pierce armour and shot it at Tiraka. The arrow zoomed right through the protective gear of the fast-charging demon and into his left shoulder. Taken aback, and howling in pain, Tiraka fell to the ground.

Virata too was surprised. No asura other than himself had ever managed to knock Tiraka down. "Looks like these puny children have more power than you, Tiraka," he laughed. "Are you sure you are up for this, or shall I finish the job myself?"

Tiraka got up and pulled out the arrow. "It looks like these kids have learned a couple of tricks, but I'll soon show them," he snarled.

Now it was Virata's turn. Advik launched an exploding arrow right at his face. The demon saw it coming and snatched it mid-air. He was about to break it contemptuously into two, when the arrow exploded, blowing his right arm off. Virata dropped to his knees, screaming in agony. Dropping his gurz, he clasped the gaping wound from which the green fluid gushed out.

The two formidable asuras were shocked to realise that they were in for quite a different fight from before. The children had upgraded their arsenal, and crushing them wouldn't be that easy of a feat that they wanted to believe it would be. But failure was not an option. Harkasura was waiting. The asuras looked at one another and returned to the offensive.

Tiraka ran towards Advik, who reached for another arrow. But just as he took aim, Tiraka was onto him.

"Tiraka! Look over here, I'm waiting for you!" Riya called out. Tiraka wasn't a quick thinker, as she had told the others, and she counted on confusing him. Sure enough, hearing his name coming from someone he couldn't see, Tiraka was distracted. As he looked for Riya, hidden among the leaves, she hurled her spear at him. It caught him in the centre of his chest. Tiraka buckled over, getting his horns stuck into the trunk of the tree. His scream rent the air.

Virata, meanwhile, swung his gurz at Advik. But with the fear of failing Harkasura again, as well as the pain of a severed limb, his judgement was clouded, and the raven-headed demon had come too close. Advik was tiny compared to him, and as the boy ducked, the poor-sighted Virata lost him completely. The gurz was stuck in the trunk of the tree where Samar sat. Seeing the opportunity, Samar jumped onto a branch that brought him level with Virata's shoulders. With all his strength, he swung his sword onto Virata's remaining arm. With the same ease with which it cut through stone, the super-sharp blade sliced through the giant asura's arm. Virata had now lost both his hands.

Green blood sprayed the floor in great spurts, some onto the children. "Demon blood smells foul. I think I'm going to throw up." Riya looked sick. Holding her nose with her left hand, she used her right hand to swing the axe on Tiraka's legs, who crumbled in agony.

Advik drew another arrow from his quiver. "No mercy for the wicked. This one is for Panditji!" He shot the arrow into the neck of Tiraka, who was trying to free himself from the tree. The arrow pierced Tiraka's neck and severed his head, and the asura's body collapsed onto the ground, his head still pinned to the tree.

Virata tried to stomp Advik with his feet, but he didn't realise that Samar had climbed on his back and swiftly pierced the sword through the back of the demon. Virata's eyes rolled, as his lifeless body collapsed. Samar jumped off before the impact and managed to land on his feet. The mighty giant had fallen.

Samar, Riya, and Advik gathered around the fallen demon. They jumped up and down with joy at their victory over these two dreaded asuras. But Advik knew that Harkasura was watching, from far away. They could sense his blazing dragon-eyes staring piercingly at them.

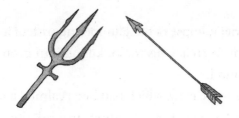

Pashupatastra

Harkasura was fuming at the defeat of Virata and Tiraka. He had given them another chance and, once again they had failed him. With no one else to vent his rage on, Harkasura turned to Sambara, aiming his trident at his throat.

"You're meant to be the smart one, but every strategy you've worked out has failed me. I have repeated time and time again that I cannot tolerate any failure and it's all you have given me! I'm beginning to wonder if I really have your loyalty, or if you want this army to fail in its conquest. At any rate, I think it's time for you to go, as you are no longer of any use to me."

Sambara fell to his knees and folded his hands. "My Lord, I did everything with the intent to serve and restore the pride of the asura clan. Everything I suggested was what I thought would work best. I agree that my strategies have failed, but I have never thought of betraying you, even in my wildest dreams."

All of Sambara's grovelling failed to move Harkasura, who blew a giant ball of fire right at him. Sambara shielded his face from the passing blaze and, when he uncovered it, caught a brief glimpse of the glimmering trident as it hurtled toward him. It struck his torso, killing him even before he hit the ground.

The demon army, which had been calmed and brought back to order, was now standing around the pair. They watched as Harkasura made a prime example out of the demon who was thought to be the wisest and most valuable of his aides.

Harkasura wrenched his trident out of the chest of his fallen adviser and held it above his head as he addressed the remainder of his army.

"As you've now heard me say repeatedly, I cannot tolerate failure. I cannot tolerate any further delays in my plans to bring us to victory. These human children," Harkasura spat, "cannot challenge me and still live. We will conquer Bhuloka, and the punishment for anyone who stands in my way is immediate and unsympathetic death." Harkasura held up his trident and spewed a ball of fire into the sky.

"Death to humans! Hail, Lord Harkasura!" someone yelled from the crowd. The others joined the chant and reassured Harkasura that they were with him. For a moment, Harkasura soaked in the chorus of war cries. Then, he raised his trident above his head, and the asuras stopped abruptly.

"Wait here. I will come back after punishing the human children," he grunted, and leaped into the air.

Advik, Riya and Samar watched as Harkasura's arrival shook the ground, a short distance away. A dragon-headed, fire-breathing demon with blazing red eyes and a trident was intimidating. The ability to fly only made him more terrifying. His lack of armour showed that he was not in the least bit concerned about an attack. And if they did attack him, he was not concerned that it would hurt enough to warrant body armour.

He blew a fireball into the air and looked them over. In his low, growling voice he said, "I don't know how you three managed to defeat two of my best warriors, but the gods will repent for helping you. I am going to end each of your lives and take extreme pleasure in doing so."

"We will see about that," Advik said, as the three stood close to each other contemplating their next move. Harkasura uprooted a large neem tree and threw it at them. It was too late to run far enough to avoid the impact, but Advik managed to release a couple of arrows to cut the tree into pieces to minimise it. Samar used his sword to cut their way out.

With a terrifying laugh, Harkasura hurled his trusted trident at the kids. But two quick arrows from Advik's new arsenal flipped Harkasura's treasured weapon in mid-air. He roared in anger, and in an attempt to rattle the children, created the illusion that trees were raining down from the sky.

Advik and Samar looked up in confusion, wondering how to avoid being hit. Riya had noticed the trees disappearing once they fell to the ground. She had figured out Harkasura's game. "Samar, Advik! He is trying to trick us. It's an illusion."

Advik paused for a moment to collect himself and then began to shoot a barrage of arrows in Harkasura's direction.

Harkasura managed to escape, but his illusion fell apart. He was angry that these children were proving to be more than a thorn in his flesh. However, this was the first time that he actually felt challenged; that someone could stand their ground against him. He almost began to enjoy himself and decided to amuse himself with a good game of cat and mouse.

He tossed whatever weapons he could at the children. When they countered everything he threw at them, he resorted to illusions. Samar was swinging his sword, and Riya was skillfully using her axe to cut out fusillade.

At one point, the children saw Harkasura lying on the field as if he were dead, and the next moment he had assumed a hideous form the size of a mountain. Advik drew an exploding arrow and shot it. The explosion destroyed the illusion. Next, Harkasura produced a huge cloud that began to dump rocks and lightning bolts. It was frightening, and the kids scurried to hide among the trees.

Harkasura was so swift with his tricks that the children had no time to think, they could only respond with whatever came immediately to mind. "This is crazy. We can't make out what is real and what is not," Samar yelled out to Advik and Riya when Harkasura had paused for a brief moment. "Advik, use the Pashupatastra. Otherwise, Harkasura will continue to toy with us and tire us out. He's playing mind games with us."

"I want to finish him off, but I can't see where he is. He is moving so fast and changing forms. We only have one shot at this and I don't want to blow it."

"There he is, look! To your right," Riya shouted.

"No, he is here to our left," Samar added to the chaos.

Yet Advik saw Harkasura in front of him. This was challenging, and he couldn't decide whether or not to draw the three bronze arrows. Suddenly, a giant creature appeared in the sky, spitting fire and blazing meteors. The thunder from the beast began to shake the earth.

One of the meteors knocked Samar unconscious. Riya dropped her weapons and rushed to his aide. As the next one hurtled toward them, Advik shattered it with one of his arrows.

Finally, Advik had his shot. As the creature in the sky morphed back to the hulk of Harkasura, he drew the three bronze arrows, closed his eyes and uttered the mantra for the Pashupatastra.

ॐ नमो भगवते महापाशुपताय तुलबलवीर्य पराक्रमाय।
त्रिपञ्च नयनाय नानारुपाय नानाप्रहरणोद्यताय सर्वांग रक्ताय।।

Om namo bhagwate mahaapaashupataaya
tulabalaveerya paraakramaaya.
Tripancha nayanaaya naanaaroopaaya
naanaapraharanodyataaya sarvaanga raktaaya.

Then he pulled the three arrows and released them towards the terrifying creature. The three merged into one fire-spewing giant arrow. It was as if everything came to a standstill; the air stopped moving as the arrow soared through the sky and struck Harkasura in his chest. There was a blinding flash of light as if a giant flashbulb had gone off. Advik fell to the ground, feeling like a strong wind had blown him down.

The lifeless body of Harkasura fell from the sky and crushed the trees beneath it. Advik kneeled down on the ground and dropped his bow to the side as he looked at the sky.

The demon army scattered in terror, seeing their invincible leader felled. They began to leap back into the crack that had been created between Bhuloka and Rasatala. Advik took a big, deep breath and looked at Riya. Samar's eyes were still closed, but they knew that he was going to be all right.

Keeping a promise

With a shower of flowers, the gods sent down their blessings. As the flowers touched them, the children felt a new rush of energy. Samar felt revived, and the three of them looked up at the sky, where the sun was rising.

"Narayan! Narayan!" Narada appeared before them, radiant in his celestial form, veena and all. "The gods are overjoyed. Advik, you — with your brave friends — have fulfilled the prophecy of the tenth son, vanquished Harkasura, and brought glory to the lineage of Karna."

"I did it for Dada," Advik reminded Narada. "Now you have to make him well. But what about Panditji? And can I keep the book of mantras?"

"My son, the Ashwinis will cure your grandfather. You can't keep the book of mantras. You wouldn't need it for anything else. You know a few but use them wisely. Who knows, some day I might hand over the books to you all again!" Narada replied.

"And Panditji?" Riya asked.

"The gods have already welcomed him into Swargaloka," said Narada.

"But what do we tell his family?" Samar questioned.

"They don't even know what he was doing with us. They won't believe that he died in a war with the demons."

"Can we have a maya take his place for a short while and pretend that Panditji died of a heart attack or something?" Riya thought it to be an excellent compromise.

"Hmmmm…" Narada mulled over the suggestion for a bit. "Okay, I think we can do that, but the maya won't last for more than a day. Given that Pandit Ramashankar is already dead, it can't be for longer than that."

"What about you two," Narada asked, looking at the twins. "Advik couldn't have done this without you. So tell me what you want, and the gods will see if they can grant it to you."

"Can I keep my weapons?" Samar piped in quickly. "I want them to be in their small form, and grow when I need them."

"Samar, can't you think about anything but fighting? You could have asked for good grades or something, but you choose weapons!" Advik pulled his leg.

"You mind your own business and get a life back in the United States," Samar snapped back.

"Guys, I think I will have to spend my whole life trying to stop you two from fighting. Grow up!" Riya said, half frustrated, half amused. Samar and Advik high-fived and pointed fingers at each other. It was a setup.

"I want to be smart, really smart — in everything!" Riya asked enthusiastically.

"Narayan, Narayan!" Narada closed his eyes and requested the gods to grant the children their wishes. "Now chant the mantra to Lord Vayu, and you'll be whisked off home to Meerut. As soon as you're back, the mayas will disappear. Remember, you wouldn't be aware of what happened with the mayas in the last three days, so be careful what you say to your parents. No point in making it this far only to blow your cover." Narada smiled and disappeared.

The children chanted the mantra and, in a flash, landed outside Advik's home. They peeked inside to find their mayas playing in the courtyard. Advik, Samar and Riya hugged each other and vowed to stay friends forever.

"Let's go in and take over our lives," Advik said and extended his palm. Riya and Samar put their palms on his. They walked into the courtyard and saw the mayas disappear before their eyes. It was strange!

About a minute later, Advik's father walked in. He looked exhausted but wore a smile on his face. It was easy to guess that he was up all night.

"Sanaa, Advik, it's a miracle," he called out. "The doctors had given up hope but then, suddenly, something happened, and now it looks like Papa is on the road to recovery! The doctors can't explain it. Thank god!"

Sanaa came running from inside the house and hugged him. Advik ran up to them but, turning, winked at Samar and Riya.

Can't bully me!

It was Advik's first day back at school since his trip to India and recess time was just beginning. He was putting his backpack in his locker when, from the corner of his eye, he saw Liam and Jacob sneaking up behind him.

He spun around and surprised them.

"Are you sure you're ready for a beat-down?!" Advik asked, with raised eyebrows, smiling...

MIDDLE READERS

The Tenth Son

Can't Stop Cody!

That Summer at Kalagarh

Dangerous Froth

No Fear, Jiyaa!

The Boy With Two Grandfathers

One World

Being Boys

This Is Me, Mayil

Mayil Will Not Be Quiet

Mostly Madly Mayil

Parthiban's Dream

Beyond The Blue River

Kabir The Weaver Poet

Just A Train Ride Away

Advaita The Writer

My Brother Tootoo

Andaman's Boy

Girls To The Rescue

Little Indians

Forthcoming

Ha Ha Hasya

To Bala, brave and beautiful

The Tenth Son

ISBN 978-93-89203-15-8
© *text* Ashish Malpani
© *illustrations* Tulika Publishers
First published in India, 2019

Cover design by Aparna Chivukula

Published by
Tulika Publishers, 305 Manickam Avenue, TTK Road, Alwarpet,
Chennai 600 018, India
email reachus@tulikabooks.com   *website* www.tulikabooks.com

Printed and bound by
Manipal Technologies Limited, Manipal, India